Wildlife

a contemporary romance

Sandra Baird

Rydermoth Press

Canada

Rydermoth Press
Vancouver Island, Canada
cahoots417@gmail.com

Publisher's Note: This is a work of fiction. Names, characters, places, and incidents are a product of the author's imagination. Locales and public names are sometimes used for atmospheric purposes. Any resemblance to actual people, living or dead, or to businesses, companies, events, institutions, or locales is completely coincidental.

Book Layout © 2019 BookDesignTemplates.com
Cover Design by Club Hub Marketing & Communications
Toronto Canada

Wildlife/ Sandra Baird. -- 1st ed.
ISBN 978-1-7770351-0-5

This book is dedicated with love to my sister, Barbara, who holds the flame of hope high for me no matter how dark the way.

"I cannot choose to be fearless, but I can choose to be brave."

K.M. Weiland
www.kmweiland.com

contents

Chapter 1

Fee awoke to the hot sun beating on her face and the soft touch of someone running hands over her body. Her arms were raised then laid at her sides, her thighs grasped, and her knees bent. As the hands began unbuttoning her shirt, she opened her eyes. Dark amber male ones gazed into hers. A man kneeled beside her.

"Don't. Don't." Weak, Fee tried to stop the deft movement of his fingers as he parted the cotton fabric.

"Lie still!" he growled as he tested her ribs. Fee groaned in pain.

"Bruised ribs for sure, maybe cracked. There's a small bump at the back of your head.

His deep voice echoed through Fee's brain. She winced.

He leaned closer and whispered, "I'm sorry. Your head must be throbbing."

As his hot breath tickled her ear, Fee wanted to giggle. *I've damaged my brain if I find lying here helpless at the mercy of a stranger, funny!*

"I don't think you should try walking yet."

His low, intimate voice brought Fee to attention.

"What's your name?"

"Fee, Fiona MacRae. Who are you?"

"I'm Matt Bracken. Should I call you 'Fee'?"

"Yes."

"Are you alone?"

"Yes, but. . ."

He cut her off. "All right, I'll carry you back to my cabin. You can't weigh much."

He glanced over her slim body, but when his eyes reached her face, Fee flushed at the knowledge she saw in them. He had determined more about her body than her weight.

"No, I don't want to go. No!" Fee dug her fingers into the rough ground. She had to fight. She readied herself by tightening her buttocks and bending her knees, ready to kick if he tried to lift her.

Aware she had tensed, Matt tried to soothe her like a frightened wild thing. "Listen, little bird, you're not flying anywhere for a while. Don't fight me. Trust me. I won't hurt you. I'll take you to my cabin to bandage your cuts and look after you until I can get you home."

Fee glanced sideways for a large stone to use as a weapon.

"Look at me, Fee. I promise I will not harm you." The golden depths of his tawny eyes held Fee's eyes.

"I saw you fall down a steep slope and land on the dry creek bed. You may be concussed or in shock. Your ripped jeans are bloody. Plus, you've bruised your ribs. Try not to move. Please, let me help you."

His sounded so much more caring compared to his earlier gruff commands that Fee's eyes filled with tears. A rapist wouldn't explain himself, would he? Matt could be safe, although those compelling eyes made her uneasy. Was it ever smart to trust a tiger?

"Where is your cabin?"

"Not far from here, about 15 minutes. It has electricity, running water, medical supplies, and a telephone. You need to get out of this heat, Fee."

She had to trust this stranger. What else could she do? Her bruised muscles screamed, plus her head spun when she moved, making her dizzy.

"I guess I've no choice but to trust you."

He reached one arm behind her, the other arm under her legs, cradling her against his body. He stood up, lifting her as if she was a small child. She laid her head on his solid chest as his arms tightened around her.

He strode over the forest floor, adjusting his stride to the spongy layers of moss, as pine needles and twigs crunched underfoot. Swaying, he dodged branches as they swung back, combing his hair with their thin fingers. The earthy scent of decaying leaves competed with the tangy aroma of cedar.

Peeking up, Fee saw the black hair curling at the open neck of his shirt. Without thinking, she moved her hand and stroked the silky tendrils like she petted Allie, her cat. A sharp intake of breath made her look up, right into his surprised eyes.

Oops. She clamped her eyes shut and kept still. A few moments later, his pace slowed as he ducked through a doorway.

As he lowered her onto a bed, he said in an amused voice, "You can open your eyes now, little bird. We're here." He leaned over her and spread her blouse wide open, exposing her lacy bra.

Fee stiffened and tried to push him away. "Don't!" She gripped his arm.

"Please try to relax, Fee. I need to ice your ribs. I also have to roll down your jeans to clean and bandage the cuts on your legs." He kept eye contact, "When I finish, I'll wrap you in a blanket to keep you warm to prevent you from going into shock. You should drink sweet tea too."

Fee loosened her death grip on his arm but still held it. Should she let him undress her? He gave logical reasons for the necessity. Also, he knew first aid and appeared to want to help her. "Are you a doctor?" Fee tried not to sound suspicious.

"Yes, but not the kind you think. I'm a zoologist. Most of my patients are injured creatures I find in the course of my research here. Now lie still while I get the ice packs."

Fee dropped her arm and closed her eyes. She had to trust him right now because she needed his help. The cool, dim room was a relief from the hot sun, and lying on a soft bed instead of the hard ground a blessing for all her sore spots, but she had to stay alert. She wiggled her toes and swiveled her ankles, no problems there. If she needed to, she'd make a run for it.

"Don't move." Matt's commanding voice returned.

He placed an ice pack wrapped in a tea towel on each side of her ribs. Fee sighed as the coolness numbed the bruised muscles. His long, warm fingers glided over her skin, and his light touch set her nerve endings tingling. It was apparent he was at ease touching human flesh, female, as well as other animals.

She scrutinized him at close quarters. His straight nose with a small scar, square chin, full lips, and ebony lashes framing seductive eyes made him one handsome dude. She figured women rarely refused him, thus the sincere appreciation those eyes gave her petite breasts made her uneasy.

"I think I can manage my jeans, so you can stop helping me." She spoke, she hoped, with confidence.

Impatience flashed in his face. "You can't undress by yourself without hurting your ribs. But if you are stubborn enough to try, go ahead." He stepped back from the bed, glared at her.

Fee reached for her jean's zipper. His furry patients didn't talk back, but she wasn't following his orders. He had better get that straight right now. As she inched her zipper lower, her cheeks burned. Was embarrassing her punishment for disobeying him? An attempt to rattle her?

Determined, Fee tensed her muscles to raise her hips to slide off her jeans, but sharp pains shot through her ribs, making her gasp and collapse back onto the bed.

"Satisfied? Or do you prefer to worsen your injuries to protect your modesty?"

"Your bedside manner needs work. Your usual furry patients don't realize you're rude, but I'm sure you frighten them."

He scowled at her.

She hastily added, "But since I need your help, I will overlook your behavior. Please help me pull down my jeans." She checked to see if her begrudging request for help had pacified him, but his expression made her uneasy. What was he thinking?

Unhurried, he bent over her, his hand tilted her chin up toward him. His face came within inches of hers, "Are you sure you'd prefer a different bedside manner, little bird?"

To avoid his eyes, Fee focussed on his mouth — his sensuous mouth. She had a wild wish to have him kiss her — a sign of a brain injury, for sure.

The corner of his mouth twitched in amusement, "Be careful little bird. Wishes come true sometimes." He traced her cheekbone with his fingertips like small flames stroking her face.

Shifting his hands, he slid them inside her jeans at her hips. He rolled her jeans, cupping her bottom to peel them to her ankles, his palms gliding on her bare flesh. Fee drew a deep breath at the sweet sensations.

"Good. You have no deep abrasions, Fee. These should heal in a few days." As he sponged the cuts above her knees, the water dripped down her inner thighs. He patted them dry, his fingers stroking her tender flesh.

Fee barely resisted moaning. Sweet Mother, this man was good.

At last, he applied the dressings and bandages, his hands brushing her calves and thighs as he rolled her jeans back up, past her lacy bikini briefs. His hand rested on her hip as he pulled up the zipper.

Her face was hot as she realized that he was observing her, well aware of her response to his touch. As she clamped her eyes shut, a moan escaped her.

His lips descended on her mouth in a delicious heat. She parted her lips for him, and his tongue teased her yielding mouth. Her fingers slid between the buttons of his shirt to stroke his chest hair. Heart racing, Fee reached up and pulled him closer, but as the rock-solid wall of his chest pushed against her breasts, pain from her bruised ribs jabbed her like a needle. Her eyes flew open as she groaned in pain. Matt pulled away, releasing the pressure.

"Forget that I kissed you, Matt. I didn't mean to, probably due to the blow to my head. I want to go back to my camp, but I'm too weak right now—give me a few hours to rest, and I'll get out of here."

She sank down into the pillows to allow the pain to subside. Matt Bracken stared at her like a man awakened from a trance.

"You're injured. I shouldn't have done that. Let's try to get through tonight with no further incidents." He stuffed pillows behind her neck to support her, checked the ice packs were still in place, stood up, and covered her in a fleece blanket. He stepped away from the bed — a man distancing himself from temptation.

"I should leave..."

"You're in no shape to go anywhere tonight, but I will get you back to your camp tomorrow morning. Fee, I'm sorry. I promise I'll behave myself tonight — no matter how enticing the invitation. Rest. I'll make that tea."

Reassured by his apology, Fee made her expectations as clear as a mountain stream. "I'm willing to stay here for a while, even the night, but I'd appreciate it if you'd keep your opinions to yourself — and your hands too!" Her breath caught as she recalled the delicious sensations those hands created.

A throaty chuckle brought her back to reality, but before she could respond, Matt turned away and walked to the kitchen. Fee saw his shoulders shaking. Was he laughing?

Sure, the guy was 'bootylicious,' but he was also a severe pain in the butt. Why was she hell-bent on making a complete fool of herself with him?

In a few minutes, she was sipping the sugary hot tea Matt had brought, being careful to point the mug's handle toward her. Unable to stay awake, she drifted off to sleep, vowing to wipe that smirk off his face.

Matt stepped outside into the fresh evening air and stood by the woodshed. His arms crossed as he stared back at the cabin. *Get a grip, man. You've been in the woods alone too much if you're thinking of seducing this feisty little firecracker. Yeah, she's hot as hell, with that copper hair tumbling to her ass, those perky breasts — and skin so silky my fingers ache to stroke it everywhere. When I ran my hands up her beautiful legs to her thighs, I wanted to strip off those tiny bikini panties and find out if she is a genuine . . . Oh, hell! This woman is tasty — and a distraction I don't need.*

With no relationship demands on his time, he'd been able to advance his research on the burgeoning elk population in Banff. Why didn't the predator population keep the elk numbers in balance? He needed to stay focused.

Chapter 2

T he room was darker, and a fire crackled as Fee opened her eyes. She glanced around the log cabin. Although rustic, it had all the equipment needed for an extended stay, including a wood stove and a fireplace with a couple of comfy chairs, even rugs. He had his computer plugged into a power generator. Was that a refrigerator and sink next to it? This cabin made the small one Parks Canada lent her look like a shack. It didn't help that her photography and art gear took up most of the space.

A shadow blocked the firelight and moved toward her. Alarmed, Fee shrank back toward the wall next to the bed.

Matt scrutinized her. She looked confused, afraid. Did she have a concussion? "Don't worry, Fee. You're safe. Do you remember me? I'm Matt. I saw you fall off the overhang. You were injured. I brought you to my cabin to help you."

He bent over her face, those tawny tiger eyes watching her as his full lips curved in an invitation. He was close enough that her nose filled with the minty tang of his shower soap.

Oh, she remembered him all too well. She needed to stay sharp and focused around this sizzling hot diversion. She had to be in absolute control.

Fee tried not to meet those seductive eyes by concentrating on his square chin.

"Do you need a reminder of who I am?" His eyes measured her response.

Like a magnet, his enticing lips drew her own to part in anticipation. Fee sank back. Crap, she'd nearly kissed him again. His teasing smile caused her to pull the blanket up to her chin.

"Yes, Fee, I see you do recall our earlier . . . encounter. For a minute, I worried you had more than a slight concussion. Based on your earlier responses, I didn't think you had a serious head injury, or I would have evacuated you to the hospital."

Matt chuckled. He couldn't help himself. It was too easy to tease her, creating such pretty peach blushes. *Yeah, enough fun to lead to complications. Back the hell off. Keep it professional, you idiot.*

His voice became firm, reassuring. "As a precaution, I've contacted the Banff Park Emergency Services. They'll have someone here in the morning to examine you. You need to stay here tonight." He saw her stiffen ready to protest.

"Fee, you're free to leave tomorrow once you've been examined by the paramedic. Stay here tonight. It's not safe for anyone to wander around the reserve alone at night, especially someone injured and unarmed. Larger predators hunt at night. Or you might bump into an elk that resented your intrusion. Plus, there's a good chance that you'd injure yourself anew, even fall off another cliff, this time a much higher one."

Although his argument seemed to make sense, Fee knew better. Her research had indicated he was exaggerating the danger in this part of the reserve close to the town. Those larger predators were further in the zone.

"All right, I'll stay the night. I do need to recuperate before I hike back. It makes sense to have the paramedic check me out too."

"I'll see you back to your campsite tomorrow morning and help you pack. How did you miss all the restricted area signs warning campers that Zone R-1 is prohibited?"

"I'm not a camper. I'm an artist commissioned by the Government of Canada to create a collection of wildlife art. I'll be here for two months, possibly through fall."

"What? You plan to stay here?" Matt backed away from her, his voice tense. "I don't know which bureaucrat you charmed into giving you permission to be here, but you're not staying."

"The Director of Parks for Alberta gave me approval," Fee huffed.

His voice rose, "I won't allow you to charge around, wrecking my study blinds, disturbing the animals, interrupting my research, and requiring rescue daily. Plan on leaving this zone tomorrow because you will be!"

He moved closer to the bed, glaring down at her.

Fee stared back up at him, and, as usual, when she was frustrated or angry, her eyes filled with tears. *Damn.*

Matt's face softened. *Oh, God, I've frightened her— more proof that she shouldn't be in the wilderness.* He knelt down by the bed to her level, speaking slowly to help her understand him, "Look, I'm sorry I raised my voice, but you can see this is the wrong place for you, Fee. You can create your little pictures anywhere, even by watching a film on Banff's wildlife at the Nature Center."

The volcano building inside Fee erupted. "Get away from me, you moron. My 'little pictures' as you call them are as valuable as your research. Through my art, children will come to respect wildlife and want to protect their natural habitats."

Fee paused for a breath and then fired another shot. "I have as much a right to be here as you, and I'm staying —

and as far as anyone charging around frightening the wildlife, a big moose like you is much more of a menace!"

She shoved Matt hard. Off guard, he lost his balance, sprawling on his backside. Her anger overrode the rib pain, but it became pure fury when she heard what Matt was doing. He was laughing uproariously *at her.*

She locked her eyes shut and willed him to go away. Even a saint would hate this jerk.

Matt couldn't help himself. With the firelight catching strands of her red hair and her intense shining eyes, Fee looked just like the young red fox that shook with anger today when he untangled it from wire mesh and set it free. But with those big, smoky eyes, plus vixen hair, she was "foxy" in a whole other way. *Get a grip. You want to convince her to leave the zone, not seduce her or insult her. Idiot.*

He stood up in a fluid motion, about to offer an apology, when Fee ground out her challenge. "Trust me, I'd be overjoyed to never see you at all, but you will not make me quit this assignment. Plan on that!"

Shouting those last three words almost killed her ribs, but worse was the realization she had to go to the washroom. Her full bladder was insistent for relief, and right now, she had a more pressing need than setting Matt straight. Why did she drink all that damn tea?

She tried to push herself up from the bed but fell back, the pain from her ribs making her helpless. Fee held up her hand. "Before you say anything else, Matt, I need you to help me stand up. I want to go to the washroom." Her voice was quiet, controlled, no point letting him see how much it annoyed her to ask for his help.

Matt suppressed his desire to laugh at her attempt to control her temper. No use throwing fuel on the fire. "Of course, I'll help you. I'm sorry I didn't think of that. Because I have a septic system, I have indoor plumbing."

Matt spoke in a courteous voice. He, too, could exercise self-control. He bent his athletic body forward, his muscled thighs tight in his jeans.

"Let me get my arms around your shoulders and, if you can sit up, we'll swing your legs onto the side of the bed." As his arms embraced her, he pulled her toward his chest, and his clean, scent of soap and wood smoke filled her nostrils. She closed her eyes, inhaling. He exuded pure male. Her forward motion caused her to brush her lips on his neck, and she heard his quick intake of breath.

His voice was strained when he asked, "Are you ready to swing your legs over the side? We'll go slowly."

Fee leaned closer as she prepared herself for the pain that was coming. The action caused her lips to press against his jaw.

"If you're totally ready?" The mocking tone was back.

"Go ahead," Fee squeaked. Oh, hell, was there no way to avoid making a complete fool of herself? The scent of this guy should be illegal.

One arm gripped her hip, steadying her to sit upright, his other arm slipped under her thighs, each finger a lightning rod shooting fire straight to a place in her anatomy where it had no business going. Gradually he moved her legs off the side of the bed.

"Are you ready?" Matt scrutinized her face, his eyes unreadable.

"Let's get going," Fee ordered, her cheeks flushed. She wasn't sure if she heard a low chuckle or not.

"I'll keep my arm around you as you walk."

When they reached a doorway, Matt turned on a light revealing a modern bathroom including a shower-tub combo. With the door shut, Fee gripped onto the sink, catching her breath. She stared longingly at the tub. What she wouldn't do to sink into a fragrant, steamy, hot bath, loosen her tight muscles and soothe her bruised ribs.

Her mind drifted to a fantasy — Matt kneeling beside her, stripped to the waist, revealing his toned chest, his strong arms soaping her back, his tongue licking the nape of her neck, then his fingers trailing over her . . . When did she turn into a sex fiend? One week in the woods, and already she was going all horny bunny. Her fantasies around that man were out of control. The sooner she didn't need his help, the better.

_*_

The firelit room was extra murky after the brightness of the washroom. She should have left the light on. Barefoot on the cool stone floor, she focused on the next step and slammed right into Matt. His large hands went out to catch her, landing firmly on her breasts, cupping them like they were sparrows.

For a moment, they held the pose, then both began to move at once. Matt moved his hands to her shoulders, and Fee stepped on his toes.

"Let go! Oh, sorry . . ."

"Sorry, here let me help . . ."

Finally, Matt swept Fee up in his arms, marched across the room, and plunked her down on the side of the bed.

"Do you mind? I can walk, you know." Fee tried to slow down her breathing. His touch stirred her, awakening a need — one she wasn't planning on satisfying with him.

"It's difficult to walk in an unfamiliar room lit just by firelight. Now that it's night, I'll turn on the camping lanterns."

"Why don't you switch on the lights for Pete's sake?" Fee asked peevishly.

"I'm conserving the generator power for my computer and refrigerator. Before now, the evening shadows didn't cause a collision with such a delectable obstacle." He grinned at her, quite unapologetic.

Fee could still feel his searing fingers on her breasts. She wasn't about to talk about that!

"Can we move on? Do you have any food in that refrigerator? I'm starving." Fee didn't care if she sounded testy as long as she changed the direction of the conversation.

Matt smirked at her tactic. "I hate to leave such a fascinating topic, but, yes, I'm hungry too. I think I can manage ham sandwiches and tomato soup. Okay?"

"Thank-you, that will be fine." Fee responded primly. She tried to lie back down on the bed but ended up flopping back with her legs dangling over the side. She glared at Matt, warning him not to make a move to help as she lifted her legs onto the bed, one at a time. Pleased with her success, she closed her eyes, exhausted.

Matt watched her breath become regular, her chest lifting and falling rhythmically before he shook himself into action. She was calm now, and *he would do well to stop watching her chest.*

The scent of tangy tomato pulled Fee out of her dreamy sleep. The soup was in a cup on the side table, making it easy for her to drink, and the ham sandwich was cut into quarters. Hunger made her eat, but fatigue won, her eyelids drooped shut.

Matt walked softly over to the computer, sat down, brought up the search screen, and entered, "Fiona MacRae."

Chapter 3

The whitebark pine outside the window cast a shadow in the sunlit room, as early morning sunbeams danced on Fee's face. The rest had eased her headache, but when she swung her legs to the side, her bruised ribs reminded her they needed more time to heal. Despite the pain, she could now walk without help. A folded blanket and pillow on an armchair by the fireplace told her where Matt had slept.

Matt sat at the computer, absorbed in his work. He was reviewing what he had found out last night. He had underestimated Fee. Not only was she a wildlife artist gaining attention, but her project in Banff was the subject of a recent magazine article. It stated she gave her art a top priority in her life. Fiona MacRae was a woman who put career opportunities ahead of anything else — like his mother had done.

When Natalie Bracken had received an offer to head up the Natural Science Institute in California, she left her husband and son, but took his little sister, Babs, with her. It was supposed to be a temporary move, but a year later, when she accepted a permanent contract, his parents divorced. Eleven-year-old Matt and his heartbroken father lived in a house devoid of joy, where they sat silently at meals as if waiting for the light and love to come back.

Matt, while building his teenage body into a fine, muscled specimen, had also built a steel wall around his emotions — no admittance. As an adult, he'd enjoyed several relationships with women, but he issued no one-way ticket to his heart. Enjoy the trip, but don't plan on a permanent stay.

As the computer screen displayed his search results on Fee, a light touch on his shoulder made him turn.

"Sorry. I spoke to you, but you didn't hear me. I guess sticking your nose into my personal life is compelling reading for you. "

She stared at him, a thick, wave of sleep-tousled hair tumbling over one eye.

Matt winced. Since when was researching a person's background a crime? Still, he was an imbecile for being obvious.

"I like to have some information about the women sleeping in my bed." He stood up and switched off the computer. His eyes drifted to her torn jeans, then to her lacy bra outlined by the thin fabric of her cotton blouse. She was tempting, even in the morning.

All 5'3" inches of Fee radiated indignation with her hands on her hips. "If you have finished leering at me, I'd like to get back to my cabin. The light today will be great for my photography. I've already lost a day's work."

"Wait until the paramedic has checked you out. She'll be here in a few minutes. My recommendation will be that you leave here, return home to Calgary to recuperate. You're not in a fit condition for the wilderness."

Fee bristled at him. "Don't you dare exaggerate my injuries to get rid of me. I'll be the judge of my condition, not you. This isn't the first time I've bruised my ribs. I can handle it."

A cough caused both of them to swing their heads toward the front door.

"Hello? It's Bonnie Ryser. I'm the paramedic from Banff Emergency Medical services." A tall, middle-aged woman encumbered by a backpack stood in the doorway. She walked into the room, glancing back and forth between them.

"Actually, I'll be the one who decides what treatment Miss MacRae requires. Could you step out while I do my examination, Matt?"

She smiled at the two contenders. Tension fizzed between them. She'd met Dr. Matt Bracken before now. His rugged, roguish sensuality had caused a stir among the female staff at the Admin building when he made his rare appearances. However, anyone who refused him a request tended to regret it. This little red-headed gal needed to be a lot tougher than she looked to win a battle with him, and it was apparent a war of wills was being waged.

"My recommendation is that you keep your activities light for the next week, no hauling heavy photographic equipment. Use the pain killers when needed for your bruised ribs. Your cuts are healing well, nothing serious there. Although there's a slight swelling at the back of your head, your reactions are normal, including pupil response. I think the fall stunned you, but you are not concussed." She smiled at Fee, "I'm willing to let you return to your cabin today."

She turned to Matt, "Can you see Fee safely back to her cabin, and make sure she has enough chopped firewood for the next two weeks? And fresh well water? You'll check in on Fee daily? Also, give her your 2-way radio call sign. Cell phone reception here can be spotty depending upon the weather."

Fee raised her eyebrows at the medic's diagnosis and request for Matt's assistance. Savoring her victory, she tried not to smile smugly at him but failed.

Matt pursed his lips together. He'd lost this round, and valuable time, but refusing to help Fee seem surly and uncooperative. Everyone doing fieldwork helped each other out in this situation. Her cabin wasn't far from his, so pleading inconvenience wasn't an option either. He'd better accept the deal and get Fee out of his bed... cabin. He was already far too tempted to seduce this little vixen.

"I'll help Fee back to her own cabin today and check-in daily until she's declared fit. Unfortunately, I'll be too busy to spend a lot of time with her, but she's welcome to call me on the radio anytime if I'm needed. Thanks for coming out this morning, Bonnie. It's a hike."

"No problem, Matt. The early morning hike from the parking lot was just what I needed. Nice to be out of the office at Emergency Dispatch and into the fresh air."

She turned to Fee, "It was nice to meet you, Fee. Take it easy for the next while, and you should be fine. You can rely on Matt." Bonnie packed up her medical kit, refilled her water bottle, and stomped off up the trail.

Chapter 4

Matt glanced at the petite, curvy figure stumbling by his side. She wasn't giving up her victory with the paramedic, but this was ridiculous. He had to admire her stubborn persistence, but enough was enough. Fee had rejected his offer of a supporting arm around her shoulders while they hiked. Now, her hair stuck to her forehead with perspiration, and each step was a great effort.

The distance to her cabin wasn't great, but it was on rocky trails and often through deep thickets of tall pines. Each time she grasped a steadying branch, Matt saw her grimace as her bruised muscles protested.

"Fee, it's another quarter mile before we reach your cabin. Let me carry you. You're aggravating your bruised ribs." He reached out and put a hand on her shoulder as she tensed, then slumped in defeat.

"I guess I should go easier on my ribs," Fee conceded, and when Matt lifted her, she sighed wearily as she leaned her head on his chest, putting her arms around his neck. She breathed in the scent of lemon-lime soap wafting from his skin while his cotton shirt caressed her cheek. She wasn't sure, but she thought she felt him kiss the top of her head like he was praising a child for good behavior. She was too exhausted to protest.

A wave of protectiveness for Fee caught Matt by surprise. Not good — not good at all.

—*—

No matter where Fee found herself, as long as she was surrounded by sketch pads, pastels, pencils, and her camera, she felt at home.

She grimaced as she studied her project plan on the wall. Recovery from her injuries was going to cost her precious time needed for photographing and sketching over two hundred different species of animals, birds, and insects.

Today's hike proved that she was in no shape for the climbing and hiking needed to find most animals. Experience taught her that animals don't come parading up to her door. She had to seek them.

After Bonnie left, Matt had been straightforward in his demands — Fee wasn't welcome where he was doing his field research. He had brought out a map of Zone R-1 and circled the areas she wasn't supposed to go. If it were up to Matt, she'd hardly be able to venture out past the clearing in front of her cabin.

"You must be joking. I can't complete my project without going to the habitats and hunting territories of larger predators, including wolves and cougars. My drawings are of habitats as well as the animals; therefore, I have to be there. Furthermore, I've had fieldcraft training. I am not an amateur."

"I doubt that I'm underestimating your ability to cope with animal attacks. What's your plan if charged by an elk or stalked by a wolf?" Matt crossed his arms, confidant that Fee was a clueless amateur.

"Elks aren't going to charge me unless I threaten them or they're in rut, which doesn't happen until autumn. It's summer. Also, they wander up to my cabin already."

"And wolves?"

"Wolves will avoid me. They're more interested in the abundant, easy prey available in summer. If it were winter, I'd be cautious and not venture out alone and unarmed in their territory. The wolf I'm in danger of being stalked by has two legs."

She'd looked pointedly at Matt. He didn't even have the grace to blush. Instead, he glared at her.

The thud of an ax and the shotgun sound of cracking wood brought Fee's awareness back to the

present moment and where she was now. Her curiosity was rewarded when she glanced out the window toward her woodpile.

Stripped to the waist, Matt worked up a sweat as he split the large logs into firewood. As he swung the ax, he let go of his frustration. If he kept working at this speed, Fee's supply of chopped wood would last her the entire summer.

Through the cabin window, Fee savored the view. *God, that man is beautiful.* His naked back glistened in the sunlight, his toned muscles rippled and clenched as he swung the ax and drove it into the wood. His tight butt moved with the rhythm. It was like watching an erotic male dancer tease the audience. Fee's face flushed, and her nether region got ready for a party.

The sudden silence snapped her to attention. Matt paused, stood up straight, rolling his shoulders, twisting his body toward the cabin to loosen the muscles, and ended up making direct eye contact. Fee ducked sideways, but too late. She heard him chuckle at her checking him out. *Damn.*

She snatched up her sketch pad and pencil, returned to her chair, focused on getting her breathing under control. In no time, she was engrossed in the one thing that always soothed her emotions — her art.

An hour later, Matt stood in the doorway, watching Fee sleep slumped sideways in her chair, a sketch pad lying on the floor. Her pale eyelids were adorned with chestnut eyelashes that rested on flushed cheeks, full mouth in a seductive pout. Her ponytail was tangled skeins of auburn curls woven with twigs from the hike.

She was a mess, and all he wanted to do was kiss that mouth, and then nuzzle her neck, inhaling her natural feminine scent, a lethal perfume. Matt swept up her sketch pad and backed out the door. He'd get a grip on his urges and then wake her.

On the front step, he sat flipping through her sketchbook. Despite himself, he had to admire all the creatures that peered up at him. These weren't the cute pictures of animals found on greeting cards. Fee had captured the likeness and spirit of them right down to the shape of their nostrils and jutting eyebrow hairs. They appeared in all their ferocity, busyness, and curiosity, not just sitting still but caught in motion.

He bet that Fee had spent many a wearisome day observing these creatures in their natural habitats. No doubt about it, she loved her work, which explained why she was hyper-aware of him. Perhaps it was her natural inquisitiveness . . . *Who am I kidding? There is a heat between us that goes beyond mere curiosity.*

"What do you think of my 'little pictures' now?"

Matt shut the book and rose to his feet. He was always caught on the wrong foot with this woman. Now he felt like he was snooping.

"Your pictures are quite accurate. I admit that you're an excellent observer." He looked into her eyes, challenging her.

Fee at once flashed back to what she'd observed of him chopping wood. She saw a slow smile form on his lips. How did he know what images of him were stuck in her mind?

"It's my turn to ask if you like what you see." Matt moved closer, reached out, and stroked her cheekbone with his thumb. His tall frame towered over her as he bent his head and tipped up her chin. As his lips descended on hers, he lifted her and carried her inside to the chair, sitting with her on his lap. His mighty arms encircled her as his tongue slipped between her lips.

Fee moaned, spurring his kiss to become demanding, more consuming. As his fingers slid to her breasts, feathering them through the thin fabric, the buds firmed and begged for more. Fee slipped one hand inside his shirt, stroking his hard contours while her other hand trailed up his thigh to his arousal. Her whirling senses spoke wickedly, *go with this, let it happen*. Matt's hand slid up her leg.

Abruptly he stopped kissing her and drew back, his breath rasping. He groaned. Fee opened her eyes and met his gaze heated with need.

"This is a bad idea. I shouldn't. I'm sorry, Fee. I'll leave." He stood up, transferring Fee from his lap onto the chair. "You have a full container of well water by the door and chopped wood on the porch. I'll come by tomorrow to check on you. My radio is on if you need urgent help." He turned and strode out the door.

Fee watched his retreating back as his strides took him across her yard, and he disappeared into the woods.

She sat, staring into the forest as her breathing slowed.

Matt's rapid pace sent small inhabitants into a frenzy of scolding as squirrels and birds chattered and squawked at him from their high perches.

This was his fault. He meant merely to tease Fee, but hell, when she responded to him like that, he wanted to take all the sweetness her body was offering.

What was he thinking? That he'd have sex with her, then go freely on his way tomorrow? Fee wasn't like the women he preferred to bed. A tumble or two for mutual enjoyment, no strings attached wasn't in her playbook.

Worse yet, he was already too protective of her. She drew him to her in a way that puzzled him. Hell, he might end up getting involved with her, the ultimate screw up of his plans. He needed to concentrate, keep his focus razor-sharp on his research. And he sure as hell didn't need Fee for anything.

Matt arrived at his cabin in record time. He picked up his radio and called the Banff Park Emergency services and asked for Bonnie, the paramedic, to change the plan for him to check-in on Fee. It wasn't his job. Also, his work right now was far too urgent for him to be playing doctor with Fiona MacRae.

Chapter 5

After Matt stomped off like a demon from hell was after him, Fee was too agitated to sit down. She organized her art supplies with a fury. *The bastard! To tease me like that, and then literally drop me like I was a scorpion. It's not like I started it after all…well not totally. Okay, I didn't say no, but, for God's sake, who would? The man is hot sex on wheels.*

Of course, she knew better than to count on anyone sticking around for long. A childhood of being raised by short term housekeepers, plus an absent older brother at university, had taught her that lesson. And if that wasn't enough, her two previous and only relationships had ended with the guy blowing town. Nick, her high school crush, hit the road with a rock band, and last year Scott had accepted an offer as a comic on a cruise ship line about as far away from the prairies as possible.

Not for the first time, Fee cursed the passionate nature that led her to put her pride and heart at risk. She'd decided that her love life from now on needed to be limited to brief flings, although she hadn't even had one yet. If her response to Matt was any sign, she was overdue to try one — but not with him.

She'd keep busy getting ready for tomorrow. Her plan needed modifying to allow her to stay close to her cabin for a week. It was possible to do her preliminary photos and sketches of rodents here. There were 19 different rodents, including chipmunks, squirrels, mice, voles, muskrats, and porcupines. She should be able to find them close by.

Yesterday, when she'd fallen off the rocky overhang, she'd been observing a small female packrat. Fee smiled as she sketched the cartoon-like large, rounded ears, and the elongated, bushy tail on the tiny body.

She was buried in her work by the time the starlit sky filled the window. Her pencil flew across the page as the little creature sprang to life.

Fee rubbed her eyes. Her art had always soothed her wounded heart as a child. She hoped it wouldn't let her down tonight as she tried to push Matt out of her mind.

She dreaded tomorrow when he checked in on her, as promised. She'd have to control her temper somehow — and any other part of her that wanted to overreact.

— * —

Matt finished washing the few dishes from his canned stew supper. When he got back from checking his cameras for that night's recording of wolf pack #2, the closest pack to his cabin, he had busied himself getting a fire going, and tidying.

He had added Fee's shower towel to the laundry but hadn't changed the bed yet. As he was about to pull the pillowcase off, he sunk his face into the pillow, hoping that Fee's scent lingered. He ached to embrace her naked body to bury his nose between her breasts.

He needed a distraction tonight. His body was still in ignition mode from today's halted lovemaking. Damn. He had started a seduction with Fee that his mind said 'no' to, but his body said 'full speed ahead.' He didn't trust himself around her. Even away from her, she'd pop into his mind, interrupting his concentration.

He tore the pillowcases and sheets off the bed. The women he got involved with didn't stay on his mind. They were a brief distraction, easily forgotten as he immersed himself in his current research. They expected nothing more from him, which was the way he liked it.

He had telephoned Bonnie to back out of his daily check-ups on Fee, but no one was available to replace him. Although Bonnie apologized, he had the impression that she enjoyed his discomfort. He wasn't sure if she bought his excuse of too much work either.

Consequently, he wasn't escaping the fiery temper that awaited him tomorrow. A traitorous part of him whispered how alluring Fee was when she was as angry as a wasp.

— * —

Fee's legs stretched out in the bright sun's warmth. As she sat on her camp stool, a gentle breeze played with her hair while the sun ignited the strands to polished bronze.

She basked in the heat as sensuously as the garter snake she studied. To Fee's delight, it had slithered out from behind the woodpile this morning, a white stripe on its back, two orange ones on each side, accented by rows of black spots. He was a handsome fellow, and on her list too.

Matt stood at the trail-end, observing Fee. She was like a wood nymph charming that snake. Her shapely legs extended from her brief shorts, her head tilted to the side, and her fire-bright hair added to the effect. None of the women of Matt's acquaintance would be that comfortable sitting close to a snake, even a non-poisonous one.

"You can add snake charmer to your resume, I see."

"Yes, I seem to attract snakes today." Fee turned toward Matt and gifted the towering specimen of male arrogance with a brilliant smile.

Damn, he knew already that Fee was a smoking hot gal, but he hadn't experienced the full force of her smile, a weapon that could melt the resolve of any man. Matt narrowed his eyes in suspicion. After yesterday's rebuff, he'd expected angry recriminations, not this stunning smile.

Ignoring her snake snipe, he placed a bulging cotton bag on the porch, "I've brought you extra food supplies. I noticed yesterday that your shelves had a lot of art materials, but not much more than a few cans of food."

"Thank-you. I'm amazed you noticed that yesterday when you had so much else on your mind — and were in such a hurry." Fee's smile was sweet as she watched his reaction to her snarky comment.

Matt refused to take the bait. "I dropped by to check on you as I promised. How are your injuries?"

He crouched down to her level to look at the cuts on her legs. They were healing well. His eyes traveled up from her rounded calves to her tanned thighs. The urge to run his hands over the tantalizing curves made him twitchy. When he looked up, her stormy eyes met his. A fire was being held under tight control there. What would happen if he kissed her right now, unleashing the firestorm? He stood up hastily.

Fee jerked in surprise, grimacing with pain as her ribs reminded her that sudden moves were punished.

"Sorry. Those ribs are still plenty painful, I see. "

At Matt's look of genuine concern, Fee found her anger evaporating. "I tried washing my hair this morning, but it was too painful twisting around like that. I guess it wasn't a great idea."

"You're welcome to shower at my cabin."

The mistrust on Fee's face at the offer made him curse himself again for his behavior yesterday. "As I'm out in the field most days, you would have the cabin to yourself." Matt glanced away as an image of Fee naked in his shower came wicked and unbidden to his mind.

"You needn't worry about my injuries for two days. Someone is arriving today to stay with me. He's a doctor, so I'll be in good hands." She smiled smugly.

Matt studied her. A guy was coming to stay with her? In that small cabin? There was only one bed.

"Well, if your *needs are being taken care of*, I won't check on you for two days." He pivoted and left. Once more, Fee watched his retreat, admiring his rearview as she smiled in triumph. Take that Mr. Kiss and Run. No reason to say that her visitor was her brother Duncan. No reason at all.

Duncan's call last night was a welcomed distraction from her rehashing the afternoon events.

"Hey, Fee, how are you doing in the wilderness? Met any wolves yet?"

"Well, one rescued me, if that counts."

Fee recounted her accident, including Matt's defense of his turf in Zone R-1. She neglected to mention the embarrassing detail that she'd relished being ravished by that particular wolf.

"Fee, I have an idea. You need help for a few days, and I've finished my surgeries for this week. Time for a break, and frankly, I'd like to check out that head injury too. I'll be there late tomorrow afternoon."

His offer pleased Fee. Duncan was already at medical school when their parents died while working as botanists in the Congo during an Ebola outbreak. He'd hired a nanny and housekeeper for his 8-year-old sister. Preoccupied with his career of becoming one of the top ophthalmologists in Calgary, Duncan hadn't had much time for Fee. But, three years ago, he'd started telephoning her, meeting her for lunch, remembering her birthday, and even attending her graduation from art school.

"I'd love that, Dunc. There's just one hitch. You have to sleep on the floor plus rustle up an air mattress and sleeping bag. I just have a small single bed. Do you think you can handle that?"

"Be prepared to be amazed by my powers of endurance, little sister. You have mistaken me for a city tenderfoot." He sounded excited.

After she hung up, Fee was still chuckling at Duncan's bravado. She'd bet that a 4-star hotel was roughing it for him. An idea came to her on how to treat Matt when he did his duty check-in the next day.

WILDLIFE

Chapter 6

Matt was cursing his imagination as he unloaded his backpack, retrieving digital cards from his mounted cameras. The sealed specimens of wolf and elk scat were for the lab in Calgary tomorrow, but tonight he'd study the results of the camera's recordings.

As the afternoon wore on, he imagined Fee's greeting for her male friend. By now, the stranger was kissing her luscious mouth, the curves of her supple body molding into him. *Damn, this obsessing is insane. I need to exorcise Fee from my psyche. I'll spend the weekend in Calgary, enjoying an excellent dinner with Angelique then staying the night with her.*

— * —

Fee heard Duncan coming down the trail before she saw him. He was huffing like an elk in labor. He

staggered into the open area, wearing a backpack that would have met the needs of an arctic explorer.

"Water. . . water. . ." Fee passed her water bottle to him as he dropped the pack on the ground, collapsed onto a step, and grasped the railing.

"Nice to see you, Tenderfoot," Fee giggled.

"You won't be mocking me when you see the treasures, I've brought you from civilization." His blue eyes sparkled with anticipation behind his gold-framed glasses as he stood up and stretched to get the kinks out of his back. Fee noticed that he'd lost weight, was trimmer than when she last saw him. In his early 40's, Duncan still had his thick blond hair and rakish darker mustache. Overall, an attractive man.

"You're looking good, brother. Is there a new woman in your life?" She stepped close and patted his flat stomach in appreciation.

"A few new women, but no keepers yet. I'm glad that you appreciate my abs, little sister. It takes many bitter hours in the gym to keep away a paunch." He laughed and pulled her into a gentle, brotherly hug, his chin on top of her head. At 5'9", he still had a good 6 inches on Fee's height.

"Now let me lug this blasted backpack into the cabin. There are perishables in it. Plus, I want to examine that bump of yours."

*

The waiter refilled Angelique's wineglass as her slender fingers clasped the glass. Her deep red nails matched the ruby of the Cabernet being poured. Her navy silk dress clung to her curves as the plunging neckline revealed a heart-stopping view of her magnificent breasts.

"It was a pleasant surprise to hear from you, Matt. Did Mother Nature wear on you? The elks and wolves not enthralling company anymore?" She glanced into his eyes, stroking the palm of his hand with one finger.

"Do I need a reason to take a ravishing woman to dinner, Angelique?" Matt echoed her flirtatious tone. This was safe territory, a seduction game they played.

"You were lucky to catch me in town. I thought you were unavailable this summer. Don't tell me you miss me?" Angelique raised a mocking eyebrow.

Matt was tired of the game. A fancy dinner had been pleasant after the simple fare of his meals at the cabin, but he wasn't in the mood for the flirtatious sparring required before the evening's main event. He glanced around the restaurant at the crisp linen tablecloths, silverware, sparkling crystal glasses, and well-dressed patrons. As his eyes returned to Angelique's sleek blonde beauty, he wished instead for a shiny mess of auburn curls, a dusting of freckles on a small cute nose, and flashing gray eyes.

"Hmm, you're not thinking of me, are you? Has a woman got under your skin, Matt?" Angelique's voice

was more surprised than regretful. She had no illusions about their relationship — mutual satisfaction without any strings attached. As a rising attorney, she didn't have time for a love affair. She simply needed to scratch an itch now and then.

"I apologize for my preoccupation, Angelique. A change of scene as lovely as you should have freed my mind from a challenging problem."

She glanced at her watch. Matt Bracken was a sensuous lover, and serious eye candy, but she'd no interest in hearing about his fascinating problems with animal behavior if that was all he offered tonight.

Matt leaned over, raised her hand to his lips, kissed it.

"Will you forgive me if I make this a short night? I don't want to bore you with my concerns. I need to sort them out." He smiled at her and waved at the waiter for the check.

As he hiked home to his cabin under the midnight moonlight, Matt realized that he had to face up to his problem with Fee. Damn it, he wanted her enough to make even Angelique's charms — which were most men's wet dream — pale by comparison. Fee was a compelling attraction, and she had heat for him. Was there a chance that she'd welcome a summer fling to burn the sexual attraction out of their systems? Maybe he should find out. She wasn't as inexperienced as he first thought, considering she was entertaining a male guest tonight at her small cabin with a *single* bed. Her guest was a *friend*, but what did that mean? It was time he took action to deal with his lust before it took control of him. He strode down the path.

Laughter flitted up the trail to meet him as he reached Fee's cabin. Around a fire pit encircled with rocks, Fee and a man sat on a log next to each other, shoulders touching. The fire illuminated the affection in Fee's face. She was plainly enjoying her male company. Had Matt lost his chance with her already?

"Remember when you hid the baby tree pangolin in your room? I still remember Mom freaking out when it wrapped his tail around her ankle while she was washing her hair. I was there on summer vacation. I thought a leopard had sneaked into the house." Duncan's deep laugh echoed around the clearing.

"Peep was the sweetest little guy. He had the bad habit of wanting to curl his tail around inappropriate objects." Fee chuckled in recollection.

"He was like a baby hedgehog with a 7-inch tail. You slept with him, curled around your hand. You must have drawn hundreds of pictures of him. Ever thought of returning to the Congo? Even for a visit?"

"I don't know if I could. I was so young my memories are all mixed up. I loved the animals, and the freedom, but losing Mom and Dad like that — at 8 years old —was brutal. My memories are of a happy time, and then a sad, scary time."

Duncan put his arm around her shoulders. "I wasn't much help either. I dealt with my grief by concentrating on med school and didn't make enough time for you." He squeezed her closer.

Fee eyes dampened. Even now, it was still painful to think about her lonely childhood. "I always told my friends about my big brother, who was training to be an eye doctor. I was so proud of you."

"Well, little sister, I'm proud of you too. You're a fighter. You don't give up, and you're one wicked good artist. I've claimed bragging rights for you for a while now. Most weeks, someone tries to buy your painting of the eagle right off my office wall. Of course, my patients don't see that well."

As their laughter pealed out, Matt thought it was a good time to make his presence known.

"You two are scaring the wildlife." He stepped into view, his tall shape casting a giant shadow in the moonlight.

"Matt! I didn't expect to see you. Are you working?"

Fee looked closer at him. His jet-black hair was tousled as if he had recently got out of bed. He was wearing tailored gray dress pants, a fitted crisp white shirt that encased his biceps, and a loosened red tie. With his suit jacket slung over his shoulder, he looked even more roguish than usual. A designer cologne wafted toward her. It wasn't likely the scent was intended to entice an elk. Not hard to guess what species of animal he'd been attracting if her own response to him was a clue. Had he any takers? She'd bet he'd had offers. Why come back tonight?

"No, I am returning from Calgary. You are up late for someone recovering from injuries." He stared at Duncan.

"I had a nap this afternoon, Matt. I'm fine. Duncan is keeping a good eye on me."

"Yes, don't worry. I've examined Fee, and her hard head prevented serious injury." He laughed then winced as Fee slapped his shoulder.

Duncan reached out his hand," I'm Duncan, Fee's brother. Please join us. We made hot chocolate. Can I pour you a mug?"

Damn. Caught out. Fee had meant to swear Dunc to secrecy but hadn't expected to see Matt tonight.

Matt shook Duncan's hand, "I'd enjoy that. Thanks."

Duncan poured a steaming cup of creamy hot chocolate, and Fee popped a few tiny marshmallows in it.

"You two are used to the rugged outdoor life. I'm a city guy. All this fresh air makes me sleepy. Relax and drink your hot chocolate. Goodnight."

Duncan rose, passed the cup to Matt, kissed Fee's cheek, then climbed the stairs into the cabin. Fee noted his

impish smile as he looked back at them. Was her brother matchmaking?

Matt sat down on Duncan's vacated spot and stretched his legs out. "I haven't had hot chocolate with marshmallows by a campfire since I was a kid." He shifted the position of his long legs to a better angle from the fire and facing Fee.

"Your 'friend' is Duncan, your brother." He gave Fee a teasing grin.

Fee flushed. "Oh, didn't I mention that? Is it important?" She focused on drinking her hot chocolate.

"For safety reasons, I'd like to be informed who is in Zone R-1." Matt managed to keep a straight face though he wanted to tease her about her bluff. "I confess I heard you two talking as I came up the trail. Something about the Congo?"

"I was born there, a late-in-life baby for my parents. Duncan had already started med school. My parents were botanists fulfilling their dream of searching for an obscure plant that had medicinal properties. It's an understatement to say I was a surprise to everyone."

"You have a habit of being a surprise, Fee. It makes sense that you started out that way too." He saluted her with his cup.

Fee smiled. "Most of my early childhood in the Congo I spent by myself, hiding somewhere, watching and sketching animals, big and small. I knew where most their nests were, what they ate, and when they had their babies. The native children were too busy hauling water and doing other family chores to play with me."

Matt sat still listening, watching the emotions play out on Fee's face. "Can you talk about what happened to your parents?"

"It's been years since then. Mom and Dad both died in the early stages of an outbreak of Ebola. The authorities sent me back to Canada. Duncan, a single guy who'd never even owned a goldfish, found himself with his 8-year-old sister to look after with no relatives to help."

"There was no one around to encourage your art?"

Fee sighed. "Not really, no. I think my becoming a wildlife artist is an example of good coming out of a bad situation. As a kid, I spent most of my time alone, drawing and painting my collection of animals, including insects and reptiles. The housekeepers changed often. They tolerated the dogs and cats, but despaired of the pet squirrels, snakes, mice and beetles."

Matt chuckled. He imagined Fee as a red-headed, freckled little girl. With her stubborn nature and a love for critters, especially creepy, crawling ones, someone intent on keeping a clean house would despair. He glanced at her face, detecting that mischievous little kid still shining in her eyes.

"Fee, I'm sorry that I've been hard to get along with. Can we be friends? This is a poor place to be holding a grudge as we live in a dangerous neighborhood."

Fee laughed. "Matt, I'm not as good at staying angry as I am at getting angry. We might as well be friends. Shake, neighbor." She leaned forward, stretching out her hand.

"I have a better idea." He reached over, turned her chin toward him, and kissed her as he held her head with both hands. Her pliable lips tasted like sweet chocolate. He sighed and drew back, still cradling her face and studying her eyes.

"Next week, I'll be away at the permanent blinds closer to the mountain base. Would you like to come with me? It's an opportunity for you to sketch the big ungulates — elks, moose, and deer, plus the big cats and wolves."

Fee caught her breath. With Matt's lips so close, she was trying to shake off the desire to continue the kiss, but did she hear right? He was *inviting* her to join him at his blinds? It was a super opportunity for her to experience the animals unobserved, plus save on her ribs too because she'd be right in their habitat — no hiking to find them.

Matt watched her weighing the options. He was counting on the appeal of speeding up her project work as a carrot too hard to resist even if his other charms failed.

"I'd like that," she decided. "But isn't it too far to hike back to our cabins each day? It must be ten or eleven miles in the bush to the base of the mountain?"

"More like seventeen miles. We'll hike about fifteen miles to the platform blind and set up camp for the week. I've camping equipment stored there. Think about it. Be sure you can handle the hike, and if you can, I'll drop by Sunday evening to discuss the details."

He stood. "Now, you better get to bed. Thanks for the hot chocolate. Sweet dreams." He stroked her cheek with his thumb, gazed into her eyes, then turned and walked away. Fee listened to his retreating footsteps as he entered the forest. Her cheek tingled from his touch and the invitation in his penetrating eyes. What was he really offering?

Chapter 7

Although it felt like she'd fallen asleep five minutes ago, she couldn't resist the aroma of fresh-brewed coffee and bacon frying.

Duncan poked his head into the cabin. "Come on, Fee, I've been slaving over this hot campfire for at least 20 minutes. Your breakfast is ready."

His bustling good humor wasn't as welcome as it usually was. Fee grumbled, but swung her bare feet on the floor, and splashed water on her face.

As she walked out into the bright sunshine in her cotton sleep shorts and tee, she smiled to see Duncan sipping a cup of coffee from a chipped tin mug. No one would ever suspect that this unshaven man, wearing a wrinkled T-shirt and sweat pants with small burn holes, his hair sticking up in tufts, was a top eye surgeon. He looked more relaxed than Fee had seen him in years.

"Hey, Dunc, you're starting to look like you belong here. That bacon isn't even burnt." She patted his shoulder, plunked down on the log beside him, and accepted a cup of black coffee.

"I figured you needed an inducement to get out of bed after the night you had. Were you wrestling with a wild beast? You were flailing your covers off, flipping from side to side. Did you win the battle?"

"Not yet. Matt made me a proposition last night, and I'm not sure I should accept it."

Duncan raised an eyebrow and grinned at her. "From what I observed last night, he seems to be a reasonably civilized, good-looking guy who appeals to the ladies. You've been leading a rather solitary life, Fee. Plus, you two seem to have a fair bit in common. What's the problem? He's not married, is he?"

"No, he's not married. He offered to take me with him for a week to the permanent blinds near the mountain base. It's a great opportunity for me to have access to the larger animals in their natural habitat. I'm tempted but . . ."

"But what? You're 25 years old, a healthy young woman who hasn't taken holy orders vowing to stay celibate. Why not have some fun and get your work done at the same time? Even develop a relationship?"

"Well, I admit I've thought about a fling, but not with Matt. He's too stubborn and hard-headed for me." She didn't miss her brother's mocking smile and rewarded him for it with a punch to the shoulder.

"Yeah, all right, Dunc, I can be stubborn too. But remember, this is my chance for national recognition as a wildlife artist. What if it becomes a serious relationship and we don't make it? I'd have to get over yet another person leaving me behind. I'm no good at that. It screws me up for ages. I'm putting my career first, and that's it."

Duncan studied Fee's anxious face. "Fee, you've already achieved the status of a serious artist with the Canada Council of the Arts. That's no small feat. Hey, you're more famous than me!"

"Not around here. It seems to me more people are asking if I'm Dr. MacRae's sister than if I'm the 'famous' wildlife artist. "

"Yeah, well, my friends wonder if I can get them 'family rates' on one of your paintings because we're related. Have you checked what they sell for these days?"

He looked thoughtful and reached out and squeezed her arm. "Maybe you feel like you've been abandoned in your life, Fee, but think about it. Many romances fail. Can you honestly say that you want Nick or Scott back?"

Fee shook her head. "No! I may have bumped my head, but I'm not mental."

"And you recognize that Mom and Dad didn't abandon you. They loved you. They didn't choose to die and leave you alone. And don't forget, you still have me, and how many big brothers can cook breakfast like this?"

He poured them both more coffee and offered her a plate of overdone scrambled eggs and crispy bacon, followed by buttered burnt toast. Hungry, Fee wolfed down the food, glad she wasn't a picky eater, especially when Duncan was the chef.

"If you can tolerate more unsolicited advice from your big brother, I have a bit of hard-earned wisdom for you."

"Go ahead, Dunc. Wisdom will be a nice change from your meaningless chatter." She tried to look severe.

Duncan shook his head. "The young are so disrespectful of the wise. Fee, don't let your fears stop you from leading a full life and finding a loving relationship. Since my divorce, I've realized that a successful career is an icy comfort most nights. It won't be my number one concern if I ever find another great woman crazy enough to marry me."

It was quiet with Duncan gone. The packing up, the hilarious struggle to get the air out of the air mattress, then Duncan's futile attempts to stuff it back into its small sack had been fun. What an inept but lovable outdoorsman her brother was.

She wasn't sure she agreed with his parting shot when he said, "Go a little wild, Fee. You may find that your 'wolf' doesn't bite." Maybe she wanted to do her own share of nipping.

Part of her problem sleeping last night was the kiss had left her needing more. Was Duncan right? Should she adopt a casual attitude toward the whole sex thing?

She didn't have to get her heart involved, did she? Matt's intentions were apparent in the piercing look he gave her before he left last night. But were they? It was just a few days ago that he had bolted when they were getting up close and personal. What changed his mind? Or had he?

Was she reading the whole thing wrong, and Matt wasn't offering a physical relationship? Was it a kind invitation between friends, no strings attached? No, friends didn't kiss like that— it was without a doubt an offer of a fling. Was she ready to accept the offer? Yes, but it had to be on her terms.

What were the rules? She needed to be in control. How do you negotiate about sex in advance? She had never talked about this kind of thing with her past boyfriends. Neither of them was as complicated as Matt. Of course, they were much younger too.

A glance in the mirror did nothing to boost her confidence. Her hair was in a ratty braid, and her jeans had ripped knees. She'd start with washing her hair, and then find the one sundress she'd brought with her.

— * —

Matt hummed old tunes in the shower. Soon he would have his mind back under his control — no more distraction, no more thinking about Fee instead of his research. It was a perfect set up — a hot week together, scratching their mutual itch, getting the whole sexual tension thing out of the way. The best thing was to go with the urge and let it burn itself out, a satisfying experience, no commitment. No one's feelings hurt.

But would Fee agree to a fling? She wasn't a casual lover like Angelique. He dismissed his doubt. He wasn't an expert on everything about women, but there was no mistaking Fee's interest. This firecracker was ready to be lit. He grinned to himself.

He put on snug clean jeans, the fabric clinging to his thighs and rear. His black corduroy shirt opened at the neck, the material emphasizing his muscled arms. He might as well improve his odds.

He tried to ignore the niggling thought that Fee might refuse him.

— * —

Fee's hair glowed crimson, her off-the-shoulder jade sundress changed her gray eyes to green as her tanned shoulders gleamed in the sunlight. She laughed at herself — you'd think that she was getting ready for a first date, not preparing to have a frank talk about a sexual fling.

She walked to the small log bench under her favorite old-growth birch tree, sat down, her back resting on the massive weathered trunk as the gentle rustle of the nickel-gray leaves in the breeze soothed her jitters. She closed her eyes.

Matt stood gazing down at Fee's sleeping form. She was sensual yet vulnerable. She looked like a small woodland sprite in that filmy dress, bared shoulders, sleeping like a trusting innocent. He had an urge to pick her up and cradle her in his arms, safe from the troubles of this world. Instead, he bent over and kissed her rounded shoulder, tasting the sun-warmed skin.

She opened her eyes, her lips pouted from sleep. "Hi, Matt. This grandmother tree lured me to sleep."

She laughed up at him and caught her breath at the heat in Matt's intense gaze. She reached for him as he pulled her off the bench and clasped her in a steel embrace, his lips crushing hers. The world melted into sensation as need engulfed her. She opened her mouth to his urgency as he plunged in to taste her. Matt swung his arm under her bottom and began carrying her toward her cabin.

Fee rasped, "Wait. Stop."

"What's the matter?" Matt's husky voice echoed his frustration. He set her down on her feet and backed away with his hands on his hips. "Are you getting even with me for the other day?"

"No, it's not that at all. We need to talk about . . . well, the rules." Fee's face flamed.

"Rules? Do you mean protection? Don't worry, I'm prepared." He moved closer.

"Yes, that's important, but that isn't what I mean. Look, you've had plenty of casual relationships, but I haven't. I mean, what are the rules?"

Fee backed further away, plunked herself down on the top step to her cabin, and narrowed her eyes at Matt. Her heart was racing, and her engine was still revving to continue the sweet dance they were engaged in a few seconds ago.

Matt was unbearably sensuous with his black, tousled hair, flushed eyes and cheeks, his powerful body emoting a siren call as ancient as Adam and Eve. She was dying for her hands to stroke the curve of his thighs and taut butt. She tried to slow down her rapid breathing.

He watched her. As a man, he recognized he could have her right now. She was ready. "Well, there are no hard and fast rules, but the common understanding is there are no serious commitments expected. It's a short-term temporary arrangement, like a holiday."

He tried to read her face as she mulled this. She was quiet — not a good sign with Fee.

"To be clear, you are saying we have fun, and no one gets hurt? And we are free to end the fling any time? Are we exclusive during it?"

"Those could be conditions. It won't be forever, for no longer than the week we are away." Matt gave her his most dangerous smile, the one filled with the promise of downright dirty delights.

"After the week we go back to our earlier relationship? I mean, it seems weird." This wasn't sounding like "fun" anymore. She'd be dicing with her heart at stake, and so far, gambling with her emotions was a losing bet.

He tried to reassure her. "Weird? Not really, we'd be friends and get on with our work as if nothing had happened between us."

"I have to think about this, Matt. Does the invitation still stand to spend the week at the blind doing my work, even if I decide not to indulge in a 'thing' with you?"

A voice in her mind was screaming, *Are you nuts? Are you turning down this invitation of hot sex, for a WEEK, no strings attached, the fling you wanted?* But another voice screamed as loudly — *Don't be a fool. Protect yourself. Pain alert.*

Matt pondered his next move. This wasn't the response expected. He had never had to negotiate like this with a woman over a bit of sexual fun. The more he said, the less likelihood of Fee agreeing to his proposition. He needed a new approach.

"The invitation for you to work at the blinds still stands. It never depended on our being intimate. Let's not make rules. Let's keep our work plan for the week. It's up to you if anything else happens. Your decision. Agreed?"

"Yes. That's fair." Fee smiled, relieved. She'd be in control. She didn't have to commit herself when she wasn't sure she was ready.

"Let's get started on our lists for our backpacks." As Matt sat down beside her, his thigh rubbed hers. He itemized the supplies and equipment already at the blind. They were able to come up with a reasonable load each, although Matt's was much heavier than hers. In fact, he insisted upon carrying most of her bulky artist supplies and camera equipment. Fee enjoyed brainstorming with him, naturally touching his hand in agreement with ideas.

The sun was setting low when they finished planning. They still needed time to pack for an early start tomorrow at 5:00 a.m. right after sunrise. This meant they would be hiking in the cooler morning air, not the heat of the afternoon.

Both stood up, walking stiffly down the steps. Fee stretched to get the kinks out. The off the shoulder neckline revealed the creamy mounds of her breasts rising and falling.

Matt drank in the enticing view, leaned over, kissed her shoulder, then with the tip of his tongue lightly licked her neck to her ear. Fee trembled, her eyes bright. Matt's mouth moved to hers, tenderly kissing her while he stroked her shoulder with his thumb in a lazy rhythm.

Slowly he released her while her eyes were still closed, and whispered, "Until tomorrow. Sweet dreams, Fee." He strolled away.

Fee, with her heart beating like a hummingbird's wings, stood bewildered, watching Matt's retreating back.

Chapter 8

The royal purple morning sky faded to lilac as Matt scrutinized Fee, sitting on the step of her small log cabin with her backpack at her feet. His eyes slowly drifted down from the battered safari hat on her head tied under her chin, to her forest green and bark brown military camouflage shirt and matching cargo pants, and laced high top hiking boots. Attached to her waist at the back were a binocular case and an army canteen water bottle. On her hips, a knife sheath, bear spray canister in a holster — *and a leather holstered Glock 20 pistol*. She looked like a petite guerrilla fighter.

"Whoa, hold it! We didn't discuss you being armed. I have a rifle if needed and a license to carry it. You can't bring that gun. It's illegal. Moreover, you might end up shooting me." Matt held out his hand for the weapon.

In one fluid motion, Fee had the pistol unsheathed and pointing at him. "This is for use in an emergency. You said you'd bring a rifle, so I brought my pistol. I'm used to being alone in the wilderness, relying on myself. Unless you plan on providing constant protection, it stays with me."

"It's effective only if you can hit an animal in the right place the first time, meaning you are one hell of a shot, which I doubt." He kept his hand held out, expecting the pistol.

"As a matter of fact, I am. I'm fully trained and licensed for this pistol, as well as a rifle. You can't go wandering in the wilds as I do and not be prepared for the unexpected. I've yet to bag a human, although I've had to shoot a charging moose wounded by a hunter and, on one occasion, a rabid raccoon."

She sheathed the gun. She stood straight, steely-eyed, ready for battle.

Matt glared back at her, his square jaw rigid. *For God's sake, just when I've got this woman figured out, she blindsides me. One minute she's a woodland nymph, the next minute a gunslinger.*

"Look, this is about trust and safety. I need to trust that you know what you're doing with a weapon. Here's my rifle. If you can shoot a pine cone off the upper branch on that spruce tree in this light, you can keep the gun."

He unslung his rifle and handed it to her. Fee dropped her pack and took the weapon. Matt felt a little guilty about giving her such an unfair test in this poor light, but he needed to be sure that she wasn't a cocky amateur before they went deeper into the zone.

Fee pushed her hat off to dangle down her back by the strings, cocked the breach on the rifle stock, checked the magazine for bullets, snapped it shut, shouldered and sighted it. Squinting, she widened her stance and fired. Matt saw the pine cone fly up into the air, the crack echoing around the suddenly wide-awake forest. Forest creatures reacted with chattering shock and fear.

"All right, you can keep the gun. You're a damn fine shot. I hope that your judgment is as good."

For once, Fee had the sense to not grin as she handed the rifle back. She shouldered her pack, pushed her hair under her hat, and started down the trail.

She didn't need to gloat about reminding Matt that she, too, was a professional with field skills — and not just another woman lusting after his divine, tempting-as-forbidden sin, body. Besides, she couldn't afford to mess up this opportunity to observe those elusive predators in their natural habitat.

Matt shortened his strides to avoid bumping into her as she marched down the narrow trail. Once they left the beaten track for the less frequented areas, he'd insist on leading them.

The more he learned about Fee, the more he realized that Fee wasn't a woman to take anything lightly. Now was the time to have second thoughts while he still could. She was passionate about everything in life, which included getting naked with him.

He couldn't see her scratching an itch with him and forgetting about it afterward. The intensity that radiated from that shapely, compact body topped with fiery red hair and fueled by a fierce, sensual nature drew him.

No, if he didn't want to hurt her, he needed to resist the urge to seduce her this trip, keep his distance. But damn, he wanted her so much he felt like a hormone-crazed teenage boy.

The sunlight was filtering through the trees with a bright, blue sky winking at them between the branches when Matt called a halt by a stream.

"I usually stop here before the last part of the trip. Let's eat and rest. It's a rough trail from here on."

Fee, grateful, sank down on the nearest boulder and drank thirstily from her water canteen. The surrounding muscles of her bruised ribs were burning. She'd have to chill them down as soon as she got to the blind. Meanwhile, she wasn't going to show weakness by asking Matt to slow down and take more breaks.

The last mile, they'd spotted bear scat, and trees scarred with bear claw scratches. Both of them were on the alert. Matt sang the Canadian anthem, *O' Canada*, in an off-key tenor, while Fee joined the chorus in a squeaky soprano. Neither wanted to surprise a bear.

Matt sat across from her, keeping his rifle close by as he searched through his backpack for lunch. He'd made ham sandwiches and added a package of raisin cookies that morning with a thermos of coffee. As he was handing Fee a sandwich, he heard a huff-like low cough to his left.

He dropped the sandwich and reached for his bear spray, rising to his feet and lifting the rifle with the other hand. Facing toward the bushes, he slowly backed up. A pair of black marble eyes above a long snout was watching them, and massive shoulders could be seen above the undergrowth. This was a large bear, too curious about them.

Matt shouted, "Bear!" and raising his arms over his head, he pointed the rifle upwards and pulled the trigger. The burst of sound was like a thunderbolt, and the bear disappeared, crashing through the forest, away from the intruders. Matt stood watching and listening to the retreat. That bear was putting lots of distance between them.

He turned to Fee, but she wasn't there, only the empty place on the boulder she'd been sitting on. He spun around, but there was no sign of her.

"Up here!" Fee whispered from above the boulder. She was stretched out on a branch, ten feet up the tree with her bear spray canister aimed at the spot the bear had vacated.

"It looks like that old boy is headed for the mountains. Come on down, Fee."

Fee holstered her spray can and was down in seconds. She moved like she lived in that tree.

Matt whistled in admiration. "Where did you learn to climb like that?"

"At first in the Congo, but now I'm often in a tree when I'm observing animals. It has proven a useful skill in many situations." She beamed at him.

"You've heard that bears are excellent tree climbers, too, right?"

"Of course, but there wasn't much room here for you, the bear and me. I thought I'd be your back-up if it charged. From painful firsthand experience during field training, I can confirm bear spray works like a damn. It's incapacitating, but it doesn't kill you, even though it feels like it. Plus, from the vantage point up the tree, I had a good chance for a close blast at that big guy."

"While I appreciate your hidden skills and back-up, Fee, maybe we should spend a few minutes talking over our defensive tactics. To avoid shooting each other by accident next time?"

Fee chuckled. "Good point. I wasn't sure if you would be forced to shoot that bear. I hoped not because I'd like to sketch him if he revisits us. He's a prime example of a mature male."

She picked up her dropped sandwich bag, sat on the boulder, and munched. Excited by the bear's visit, she forgot all about her throbbing ribs for a few minutes.

Across from her, Matt watched her with amazement. She was at home here deep in the wilderness. Few people were as fearless as Fee. She was the savvy, sexy woodswoman that, until now, he thought was a fantasy — a female that existed exclusively in adventure films.

Her copper hair tumbled over her shoulders, her perky bottom rested on the boulder, and her eyes were sparkling silver pools in the glinting sunlight. He was stirred by more than admiration — a lot more if the tightening in his groin was any indication.

Matt focused on pouring them both a coffee from the thermos. When he handed the mug to her, he smiled into her bright eyes and traced her jawline with his thumb. Her lips parted, anticipating a kiss, but instead, he returned to his spot across from her and began discussing the plans for the rest of the day.

Fee wrinkled her brow. Could he be uneasy about that bear? He had to be in deep thought not to take advantage of a chance to kiss her.

Chapter 9

It was 3:30 p.m. when they made it to the blind. Two hours before that, Fee's ribs had been constant torture. The jerky motion of climbing over fallen logs, grasping branch handholds, and stumbling up and down steep ravines had irritated them. Her pack was a load of cement now.

Fee didn't realize that Matt had stopped walking as she pushed forward, her head down like an overburdened pony, one painful step at a time. She bumped right into him as he waited for her. He caught her, gripping her arms to steady her. As Matt took her pack off, she swayed from fatigue. He guided her to a fallen log, and Fee sank down her chest heaving.

"Look, Fee, you won't survive this field trip if you're stupid. I thought you were an experienced wilderness camper. You violated the first rule of survival!" He threw down his own heavy pack and handed Fee her water canteen.

She drank deeply from it. Hell, Matt was right. It was her pride that had prevented her from pacing herself, stopping and recovering. She wanted to prove that she could cope with the rigors of fieldwork. Instead, she'd acted like a rank amateur.

"In the wilderness, you have to be mindful of reaching your physical limits and make camp before you're too exhausted. For God's sake, it's the first rule of the field. Right now, Fee, you couldn't keep yourself safe. You are not thinking!"

Why hadn't he thought about her bruised ribs while they were hiking? Because he had been focusing on her hot body, shimmying like a pole dancer over all the obstacles on the path, that's why.

"We'll rest here for a half an hour and then hike slowly to the blind. It's an outlook blind with a platform, safe from the big predators here. We're deep in the zone now, and I'd prefer to spend my time collecting data on the elk and wolves rather than shooting them to protect you. It's my fault. I should never have suggested that you come with me. I'll take you back to your cabin tomorrow."

Fee's head jerked up. "You are totally overreacting. We aren't going back to my cabin tomorrow. Yes, I agree that we should have stopped earlier for me to rest. I admit I made a mistake. But I'm not helpless. You must admit I can defend myself."

Matt did not look convinced.

"What's more, Matt, I'm not alone — you're here. If I'd been alone, I'd have set my own pace and not followed yours — and from now on, I will." She glared at him.

"You may be your own boss back at your camp, Fee, but deep here in Zone R-1, I'm the leader, make no mistake. Your safety is my responsibility, and I, not you, will decide tomorrow whether you stay."

As Fee opened her mouth to protest, Matt held up his hand to stop her.

"We'll be sleeping in the high blind tonight, and you have to be able to walk there. You must rest now. I can't carry both you and all our supplies. Understand?" Matt's steely tone and glower tolerated no argument.

"Understood." Fee agreed and clamped her mouth shut before she told him what a rigid, dictatorial jackass he was. If she were willing to suffer a little pain, what was it to him? Although fuming, she kept quiet. She slipped down onto the spongy moss by the log in the shade, stretched out to ease her throbbing muscles, and closed her eyes.

Matt sat, guarding her like a rottweiler. In her camouflage outfit, her small form looked like a child's action figure flung under a tree. A smile tugged at the corner of his mouth. She could make his blood boil with fury one moment, and the next, he wanted to make slow love to her.

He let her sleep for thirty minutes, then woke her by shaking her foot, deciding not to get any closer. They finished the hike in stony silence accompanied by the jangle of the bear bells Matt had attached to their packs.

—*—

Fee was surprised at the design of the blind. It looked like a small hut on stilts. Even though the climb of the ship-style rope ladder was at most fourteen feet high, she was glad that Matt made her leave her backpack down at the bottom for him to carry.

Talk about being in good shape. After carrying a jumbo pack through fifteen miles of rough country, Matt still had energy left to get things organized.

He'd brought her chilled, wet cloths wrung out in the nearby river to ease her muscle strain and insisted that she take a painkiller and rest on the old chaise lounge garden chair in the blind. She couldn't imagine anyone hauling that chair on his back for fifteen miles, but as she sank onto it, she blessed the unknown benefactor.

Fee felt like a wimp as she watched Matt work, but she admired his sheer physical power. A gal couldn't dismiss bulging muscles, no matter how peeved she might be with the owner of them.

The platform was constructed with a ventilated roof and sliding window slats for viewing when the weather got nasty. A fresh breeze chased the stale air out through the latched open window.

"That's better. We can keep the larger beasts out, but insects and rodents sneak in through the slightest opening. We stow most gear in our metal storage chest even when we're here."

Fee had been puzzled whether the long metal box by the far wall was a table or a bed.

"Alright, if I store equipment in the chest? It will be a safe place to keep it away from a sharp-eyed crow attracted to my shiny camera lens."

Matt glanced up from rifling through his pack. "Sure, no problem." He fished out a banana and a cookie and passed them to Fee, extracting the same for himself. "This will have to do us for an hour. I need to fill the water bag at the river plus get the firewood chopped and under a tarp in case of rain."

"What can I do? I know we need to set up before nightfall when we bring up the ladder. I can't carry heavy stuff, but I can do anything else." To prove she was up for a task, Fee sprang from the chair, awaiting orders.

Matt turned toward her. He appreciated her attitude. She wasn't sulking about his earlier criticism. She took it

like a professional, admitting that she'd made a mistake, albeit reluctantly. Instead of nursing a grudge, she was trying to be helpful.

"We won't use the stove for cooking and heat unless we get rain for several days. At this altitude in the mountains, it's incredible how brisk the air can get even in the summer.

You can help out by making supper. Go ahead and use the small propane camp stove tonight, but from now on, we'll cook our meals on a campfire. Also, you better set up your equipment for tonight's work while it's still light."

"Are you saying that I can stay and do my work for the week?"

Fee held her breath. Now that she saw this place, she realized it was perfect for her to make headway with her list of must-have animals. She stayed quiet, awaiting his verdict.

"Maybe I was hasty on the trail. You deserve a chance to get your work done after enduring a lot of pain to get here. Added to that, I can't afford to lose two days to return you to your cabin and then come back here. It makes sense to let you stay."

Fee flew the few feet to him and threw her arms around his waist, wincing as she hit the solid wall of his chest. She buried her face in his shirt, the musty scent of fresh male perspiration and wood pine filling her senses.

Matt laughed and put his arms around her small waist, unable to resist her excitement. He could feel her firm breasts through his shirt.

"Thank-you, thank-you, Matt. You won't regret it, I promise. I'll follow all field protocols. You'll hardly know I'm here!"

"I doubt that on all counts." He looked down into her joyful face and bent to kiss the top of her nose and then her upturned lips. She tasted like sweet, wild strawberry, and he needed — to get the hell out of here!

Matt released her, grabbed the water bag and rifle, and bolted out the door for the river. It was futile to resist Fee. She was like an alluring siren of Greek myths, luring him into the rocks, except she seemed oblivious of her power. Even her scent was enough to tip him over the edge.

Damn it to hell. He should face it. Abstinence was no cure for sexual heat. He could have made love to Fee right then in the blind.

Bringing her here was about the stupidest thing he had ever done — unless he followed his original plan to scratch the itch and have a brief fling. But it wasn't a single itch anymore. It was now like a bad case of poison ivy — uncontrollable.

He was sure that Fee wanted him just as much. Was it a passion for him individually or her passionate nature that made her open and physical with him? Did it matter?

Fee carried her equipment out to the six-foot platform that encircled the structure. A wooden bench attached to the deck was ideal for night observation. The river wasn't far from the blind, and as a water hole, it drew all animals.

It was also a favorite nighttime buffet for coyotes and foxes, as many tasty smaller creatures were sure to show up there. Fee set up her tripod and attached the telescope. She'd keep the night vision lenses in the case until dark.

Right now, she'd check the area. She might get lucky and spot an animal she could sketch. She peered through the lens, adjusting the focus. There was the river, and Matt lounging under the tree. He wasn't in such a big hurry, after all. Fee giggled. It was hilarious when he made his hasty exits, but she had the feeling she'd have more fun if he didn't.

In fairness to Matt, he was trying to keep his word about the choice of a fling being up to her. Why hadn't she agreed right away? If possible, her attraction to Matt was increasing with proximity, likely his plan.

Now she'd be embarrassed to admit she was willing. What was she going to say, *Okay, Matt, you can jump my bones?* Was she reckless enough to 'just do it'?

No answers popped into her mind, so she focused on spotting her creatures instead of soul searching — more fun and a lot easier. Was that a badger rambling by like a bumbling professor?

—*—

80

Fee examined the treasure trove inside the metal storage box. She'd opened it to put in her camera and sketch pads. It was six feet by four feet and served as storage, a table, even a bed frame. It contained a rolled-up air mattress, a double sleeping bag — *double, not two singles* — plus a crank battery 2-way radio, and a small power generator.

Matt had thought ahead when he stocked this chest. He could survive here for an extended time with these essentials. Fee was glad that she hadn't lugged it all on that fifteen-mile trail. No one would starve either as there was a fishing rod with tackle and lures, plus boxes of ammunition for the rifle.

"Are you hungry?" Matt unslung the fully extended water bag from his back — it was now as heavy as a bag of rocks. He hung it upside down from a hook on a rafter and adjusted the spout.

He reached into the storage box and pulled out the camp stove, while Fee grabbed a pot and dishes. Soon he had the water boiling. "We'll have freeze-dried stew tonight, but tomorrow you can catch fresh fish for us."

He turned back to the stove, hiding his face. Was Matt laughing? One mistake on the trail, and now he assumed that she had no field skills at all, that catching a fish was beyond her abilities.

"No, problem. I'll catch us a trout tomorrow, maybe a brown trout or even a rainbow." Her voice oozed confidence. Matt didn't reply, but Fee was sure she heard a stifled snort.

By the time they'd finished eating and washing up, the mauve of twilight was changing to an inky purple. Fee was busy outside attaching the night vision eyepiece she'd scored from an army surplus store. She straddled the bench to check the night action, focusing the telescope down toward the riverbank.

She pulled on her fleece sweatshirt. It was colder here at night nearer the mountain base. She jumped as Matt whispered into her ear.

"I set the cameras for night recording. You might find them useful too."

The man moved as stealthy as a cougar.

His heated breath and the touch of his warm lips on her ear sent a shiver directly to her ignition button. He placed an even warmer hand on the back of her neck and continued whispering, "Sorry, I'm trying to be quiet."

Fee was sure he was purposely blowing in her ear. His skillful fingers slid inside her shirt, massaging her shoulders. Fee's tight muscles relaxed as her breathing picked up speed. She was still peering into the telescope but wouldn't have noticed if a pink fox in an orange tutu had pirouetted to the water's edge.

She choked out, "Thanks. My muscles needed that, but I have to stay focused." When his heated hands moved away, the chill returned. His last whisper brought her to full alert.

"No problem. I'll get our bed ready."

It was a slow night for action by the river. She'd seen nothing more than a few flitting bats, and a great horned owl keeping a suspicious eye on her from a nearby tree. After two hours, Fee couldn't keep her eyes open. Twice she'd woken up, her head resting on the telescope. She collapsed the scope and took her equipment into the hut.

It was gloomy inside with all the windows closed to avoid light spilling onto the observation deck. An open roof slat let in the fresh night air. A small candle was burning in a can, and Matt appeared to be already asleep in the makeshift bed on the storage locker.

He was stretched out on his back in the sleeping bag. He rested his head on his arms, his biceps like baseballs. His spiky eyelashes curled shut on his high cheekbones, a thin white scar sliced across his nose, a slight smile tilted his lips, and his broad chest rose and fell slowly. The man was a raunchy turn-on, even when unconscious. He had left room for her in the bed by positioning himself next to the wall.

The sleeping arrangements were a whole lot more intimate than Fee expected. She should have asked more

questions about the practical details. Well, too late now. She was too dead tired to wake Matt up to discuss this. In any case, she'd be awake before him because she was hell-bent on catching a trout for breakfast.

Fee shrugged out of her fleece and pants down to her underwear. She wiggled out of her bra without taking off her T-shirt. The crisp air raised goosebumps on her legs.

She tiptoed to the bed and slithered in under the covers, turned on her side, facing the windows, careful to not touch Matt. She could feel his body heat close as her heavy eyes closed.

Matt woke to a hot thing attached to him. He turned his head. A silky mass of red curls was resting under his arm. Fee's cheek was on his chest, her slender fingers entwined in his chest hair, her firm breasts pressed his side, and a smooth bare leg flung across his thighs. Fee was cuddling up to him, childlike in her sleep.

The sweet sensuality of her body caused his manhood to stir. If he'd got a definite 'Yes' from her while she was awake, he would stroke her like a kitten until she was purring, ready for him. He had tried to stay awake until she came in, but today's labor had taken its toll. Now it was too late to ask her.

Damn! Scruples were so inconvenient, but he couldn't break his promise to let her decide.

As Matt turned toward the wall, Fee made a small protesting squeak in her sleep as she slid off him, then turned onto her other side facing the window, pushing her bikini-clad bottom cheeks into him. Matt growled in frustration.

Chapter 10

Fee popped one eye open. Shadows were fading in the room as the sunrise spilled through the roof slats. She pushed the sleeping bag off and swung her legs out, her bare feet recoiling from the icy floor. It would be too easy to give in to the temptation to drop back into that comfy warmth. Matt was lying on his back asleep. He didn't seem to have moved all night.

She found her cargo pants and slid them on quickly. She flipped off her T-shirt, turned her bare back to the bed as she fastened her bra, then pulled her top back over her head. Grabbing her shirt, socks, and boots, she slipped out the door.

The low sounds of a world waking filled the brisk morning air. Fee's crunching rubber boots disturbed a few robins planning to dine on plump worms. Fee was an

'early bird' too. She'd hidden the fishing gear behind the hut while Matt was getting the water yesterday. This was a chance to prove she had survival skills. She often fished for her supper during fieldwork and was a capable fisherwoman.

In minutes, she was in the water two feet from shore, about a yard down from the shadow of the spruce tree, casting upriver, letting her line drift back down. Most trout waited for the food to come towards them. They preferred the tree-shaded parts of a river. She'd baited her hook with an earthworm.

On her third cast, she got the familiar tug on her line. She began reeling in, keeping the rod tip above her head. The trout burst through the water, twisting and thrusting its body, but it was no match for Fee. She backed up to the shore as she reeled him in, scooping up the plump fish in her net.

Five minutes later, she'd landed one more, plenty for their breakfast, and soon was stomping back to the blind, victory in each swishing, rubber boot step. A broad grin was plastered on her face.

Matt had appreciated both early morning shows. The first seen from under his eyelashes as Fee slid out of bed. He had relished the view of her rosebud nipples and creamy breasts as she peeled off her T-shirt. Her bikini panty clad rosy bottom kick-started his morning blood pressure.

A few minutes after she left, Matt positioned himself on the deck to see the second show. He had spied her fishing tackle the night before and surmised her scheme. He expected it to be a futile effort and hilarious. But, damn, that gal could fish! She was as good an angler as himself, possibly better. Also, she'd cleaned and filleted those fish, sealing the guts in a plastic bag for burial, essential in bear country — and she'd done it all with little wasted effort.

"Here's breakfast for two." Fee beamed up at him as she climbed up the stair ladder with her zip lock bag full of trout filets and wild onion she'd picked near the stream.

"I see you caught the elderly ones not awake yet."

Fee set her prized fish on the landing, walked up to Matt, and punched him hard in the shoulder. He fell back laughing and grabbed her clenched fists to block her next punch.

"Whoa, tiger. I'm teasing you. You did a great job. I couldn't have done better. It takes a real pro to fool the wily trout."

"You got that right, and as you are ungrateful, you can get the frying pan and cook our breakfast." Fee was struggling to still appear outraged, but a smile was forming at Matt's compliments.

With the bed gear stowed in the storage locker, it was a table now with the camp stove in full operation. The salt and peppered fillets were crisping in the oil, accompanied by chopped wild onion. The coffee pot was perking away on the other burner. Buttered bread was on each plate. It was a real camp breakfast, and Fee and Matt ate it with relish.

All cooking gear was cleaned and put away by 6:30 a.m. Matt filled his knapsack with sample containers and a testing kit, slung his rifle, and left. Fee perched on the bench, tracking a movement upslope from the river. She thought she'd seen a flick of a bushy tail behind a tall juniper shrub.

Her mind, however, was on a different track reviewing what had happened before Matt left.

"I'll be on the move this morning, Fee. I'll be back around 3 p.m. If you need me, use your radio. You'll be at the blind, right?"

"Yeah, last night, I was too tired to work, kept nodding off, crawled into bed before midnight. Glad I didn't wake you." Fee glanced at him. Matt's heated return gaze caught her off-guard. *He'd been asleep, hadn't he?*

"That reminds me, Matt. When you get back, we need to talk about our sleeping arrangement. You'll be disturbed by my coming and going late at night and early in the morning. Most of the animals for my study are early morning risers or nocturnal or both. I often catch a nap in the afternoon when they do."

Fiona turned away and became busy retrieving her lens case from the storage trunk. His firm fingers gripped her shoulders and turned her to face him.

"You need not worry about disturbing me, Fee. I'm a sound sleeper out here. But you're right, we'll talk later."

Matt brushed a curl from her forehead, leaned forward, tipped her chin up to graze her lips with his, and then deepened the kiss as he heard her catch of breath. Her head swam with his scent, his hard body fitting into her hers, his mighty arms clasping her tender breasts to his rock-solid chest while his tongue probed her mouth, then nibbling her bottom lip. By the time Matt released her, both of them were panting. Then he left her with a wicked smile

Fee's hands shook as she pulled the rest of her equipment from the trunk. *Holy hell, that man could kiss a grizzly bear into submission. All I want is to surrender to him. Every girl part of me is vibrating. I give up.* She grinned. She could hear big brother, Dunc, applauding her decision.

A snarl brought her back to the present moment as she saw a black-legged red fox spurt after a brown and white rabbit that was darting sideways. The fox pounced on it and snapped its neck. Fee's camera, set on rapid repeat, recorded the action in freeze frames, perfect for sketches. This cycle of life in nature was necessary for the textbook, not just pictures of cute animals.

By 2:30 p.m., Fee had recorded enough small animal behavior to keep her busy sketching for weeks, but the largest animal to visit the river was a family of river otters. The sun was high, burning the cotton fluff clouds to slender feathers, and crickets and bees seemed to be the sole creatures able to stay awake, buzzing and chirping.

She went inside, seeking food. After she'd nibbled on the last bit of leftover trout and a few dried apricots and nuts, it was time to stretch out her stiff muscles. She pulled on her yellow swimsuit and headed for the river, her hair tied in a high ponytail, and her swim shoes like rubber ballet slippers. Around her neck, a small canister of bear spray the size of a purse flashlight dangled on a cord.

Matt reached the meadow and glanced up at the blind — no Fee there manning the telescope. Most likely, she was catching the nap she mentioned. 'Time to take a quick dip in nature's bathtub as he was sweaty and hot. He set his equipment down by the tree trunk, stripped off his long-sleeve shirt, undershirt, and cargo pants, keeping on his black jockeys. The water would refresh him and wash his underwear at the same time. He eased into the icy water, ducked his head under, and then shook his hair like a wet dog. As he floated under the tree, gazing up through the spruce branches at the jay blue summer sky, he sighed in contentment.

"If it weren't for those giraffe legs of yours, I would have used my bear spray on you."

As Matt swung his head around, he heard Fee's giggle. There she was about five feet away, up to her knees in water, her yellow suit molded to her body outlining her curves, her breasts half-moons, the scoop neck barely covering her chilled, firm nipples, water rivulets trickling down her tanned thighs.

Before he could move towards her, she swam up to him like an otter, placed her lips on his ear, and nipped It. Within seconds, she was out of the river, her shapely bottom bouncing, and her ponytail swinging as she sprinted to the blind.

Damn, how could he chase her? His equipment, especially his rifle, couldn't be left by the tree. What did she think she was doing? Didn't she realize she was teasing a wolf?

Matt entered the hut with his dry clothes over his arm, his rifle slung on his shoulder, his wet underwear clinging to his taut butt cheeks, his manhood outlined. He dried himself, flexing his tanned arms as he rubbed his broad chest, and then his thighs and legs. He hesitated at the waistband of his wet underwear. Fee, still in her bathing suit, was bent over, drying her cascading hair, the towel obscuring her vision. She peeked up at him. *Oh my!*

There's a sight that's burned onto my eyeballs forever. She wondered wickedly if he might peel off his underwear.

His seductive eyes laser fixed on her, and his eyebrow rose in the unspoken question. Fee looked away — what should she say?

"I thought I would dry off in the sun on the deck," Fee croaked.

"I have a better idea."

Matt grabbed a dry towel, stood behind her, and rubbed her shoulders. Fee could feel the press of his muscled thighs, flames against her naked wet legs. He untied her bathing suit behind her neck. Fee caught the front as it fell and held it up as he dried her back in slow circles. He dropped to his knees and wiped her all the way from her ankles to her ass. His powerful fingers caressed her legs then slipped around the edge of her bathing suit by her bottom cheeks. He was so close his breath teased her wet skin.

He gripped her hips and turned her toward him. The towel inched up her legs, pushed by his firm hands, his fingers playing upon her flesh like a piano keyboard. As he reached the front, he pulled the fabric to the side, rubbing her dry, his fingers stroking her mound. Fee was panting now, her halter top falling from her hands, exposing her pearly breasts.

"Shall I continue?" Matt's husky voice vibrated on her belly.

"Yes, yes, yes!"

Matt rolled the suit off her hips to her feet, and Fee stepped out of it, now naked as he kneeled in front of her. Tenderly he parted her with his fingers, licked her dark pink labia. Fee was breathless, gasping as sensations roiled through her. She was a fire, and Matt had splashed her with gasoline. She dug her fingers into his shoulders. He stood up, and Fee grasped his wet jockeys, tugging them down his legs, freeing his rock hard staff. From the pocket of his discarded cargo pants, he extracted a condom. Fee watched as he sheathed his impressive length.

Matt swept her up and carried her to the storage locker. He sat on the edge, positioning her on his lap facing him. Pulling her forward, he spread her legs wide on his thighs. His heated eyes on her face, he entered her in one smooth thrust. With a tidal wave of hunger, Fee encircled him tightly with her legs, pushing her body into his as he claimed her lips. Their pounding rhythm was accompanied by a crescendo of moans and cries as both climaxed. A raven watching them on the window edge, startled, flew off.

They had just lain back on the beach towel catching a breath when they heard heavy footsteps on the stairs. Matt was up and into his jeans in five seconds and flung Fee her towel. She was already pulling her shorts and T-shirt back on and dragging her tangled hair into a ponytail. Her cheeks were flushed, her eyes bright.

A firm knock on the door, a brief pause, then, "Anybody home?" as the door swung open. "Oh, I'm glad I found you, Matt. I haven't been able to reach you on my radio."

A tall, blond, park conservation officer stepped into the room. His blue eyes filled with amused questioning as he surveyed the flushed and tousled pair staring back at him. This was the wildlife artist, Fiona MacRae? She looked like a poster girl for the guys' locker room. She was braless, her T-shirt wet. Her tanned, shapely legs ended in brief shorts. Her shiny gray eyes and a mass of copper curls escaping her ponytail sealed the deal. She was a centerfold material, drool-worthy.

Sharing this outlook blind with her would be like winning the lottery for a guy, although he had heard that Matt wasn't thrilled to have her working in Zone R1. Apparently, Matt had gotten over that.

"Sorry, Geoff, we were swimming. I turn it off when I am away from it to conserve power. I was about to turn it back on. There were no messages when I checked the service earlier today."

It impressed Fee that Matt sounded normal while her heart was still racing from almost being caught in a flat out, bare ass situation. How many times had he been in danger of being caught with his pants down?

Geoff stepped toward Fee and held out his hand, "We haven't met. I'm Geoff Halloran, the conservation officer for the Zones R1 and R2."

Fee clasped his hand and smiled. "Fiona MacRae. Nice to meet you." Fee used her most professional, business-like tone. Geoff shook her hand then slowly released it, looking directly into her eyes. He beamed a wolfish grin back at her. His white teeth, tanned face, and streaky blond hair gave him a surfer appearance. Fee blushed at his frank admiration. It was apparent what he was admiring through her thin wet T-shirt.

"Is there a particular reason you were trying to radio me?" Matt cut in. He hadn't missed that Geoff was eyeing Fee like a delectable morsel.

Geoff turned to him, "There's a wildfire burning in Zone R2. You won't see it from here yet, but it's pushing a lot of animals toward this area. In the next few days, be prepared to have a surge in the animal population. Elk, moose, and deer will seek higher ground, and the large cats will stalk them. Wolves too."

"What's the status of the fire now? Should we prepare for an evacuation order? I believe that we are alone this deep in Zone R1."

"You're right. You and Fiona are alone here. We're hoping that we'll be able to contain the fire with our water bomber for a day or two until the forecasted rain. The wind's co-operating at two-three miles per hour, so the spread is slower than expected."

"Then, we can stay here as planned?" Fee couldn't hide the anxiousness in her voice. Her plans for the week could literally be going up in smoke.

"There's no danger for you, Fiona. Matt's familiar with forest fire safety protocols. Don't worry, he'll keep you safe."

Fee stiffened at the idea that her concern was about her personal safety. "My chief concern is whether I'll be able to complete my work, not whether Matt can 'protect' me." She crossed her arms and gave Geoff a steely look. Matt's eyes danced with amusement. Geoff had now met the feisty side of Fiona MacRae.

"Of course, Fiona . . . ah, I better get going if I want to get back to base by nightfall." He picked up his backpack and fitted his hat on his head.

"Thanks for updating us, Geoff. I'll keep my radio on active for the rest of our field trip."

There was an awkward silence after Geoff's footsteps on the stairs had faded away.

Matt shook his head in disbelief. "That was a close call — in the wilderness, seventeen miles from civilization, and we're still interrupted by a nosy neighbor. Come here, my ravishing girl."

He spread his arms, and Fee walked into them. Matt clasped her in a gentle embrace and kissed her eyelids and then her mouth.

"I'm not sure we fooled Geoff at all. He was eyeing us suspiciously."

"Not us. *You*, Fee. I don't care what Geoff thinks was going on here — he has no proof. I've known him for a while. He's a gentleman, so don't worry about him gossiping." Matt gazed down into Fee's upturned face and smiled as he saw her relax. He felt protective again, but this time, he didn't mind at all.

His hands slid inside her shorts and down to her rounded butt cheeks, and his fingers began delicious stroking of her bare skin as he bent his head to kiss her.

"Whoa, Matt. No time to play! It's already 4:30 p.m. I need to get set up for the evening and night action. Thanks to that fire, I might have more animals to observe and photograph than usual." Fee pushed him away.

"All right, you go ahead. I'll make us supper, but I like the sound of 'night action.'" He treated Fee with one of his suggestive smiles, guaranteed to start any female engine. As the recent "action" came to mind, Fee's face got hot, Matt turned away laughing. He never tired of teasing her.

Chapter 11

By her telescope, Fee chuckled to herself as she ate the plate of food Matt had brought to her before he left on his night rounds. This fresh air and "exercise" sure worked up a gal's appetite. She gobbled down the plate of spaghetti in spicy meat sauce as fast as her old golden retriever would have.

Fee took a deep breath and exhaled. *Well, I'm in the deep end of a fling now. There's no going back, not that I want the torture of resisting the hottest man on planet Earth. If our first experience was any indicator, that forest fire on the other side of the mountain is about to lose a heat competition to us. Hot Damn.*

Matt had been sweet and caring afterward, smoothing over any awkwardness when Geoff had almost burst in on them. Having an experienced lover like Matt had advantages, and Fee wasn't about to dwell on thoughts of his other lovers. She was committed to a week of sheer sexual pleasure, no backing out.

At the end of the week, they'd both have a lovely X-rated summer memory. That suited her fine. She ignored the small, sarcastic whisper from her heart, *Yeah, sure.*

Fee kept busy recording a herd of about a dozen elk that had wandered into the meadow, munching their way to the river. They were heifers and cows who were accompanied by this year's leggy, spotted spring calves bumping their mothers' sides to catch hold of a teat. The large number of yearlings meant that the wolves hadn't culled enough calves last year. Was there was a trailing bull elk keeping an eye on his harem? She scrutinized the top of tall bushes searching for a pair of antlers.

—*—

The elk had finished grazing and were drinking, standing belly-deep in the water, but Matt still wasn't back. He should have returned an hour ago. Fee hesitated to call him on the 2-way radio. She didn't want to appear to be anxious, but still, when a person doesn't show up when expected in the wilderness, it could mean they were in trouble.

She inputted his call number.

"Hello, Matt, radio check-in."

Silence.

"Matt, it's Fee. Please check-in."

Nothing.

Now what? They hadn't even discussed a protocol for one of them going missing. Should she contact Emergency Search and Rescue? He was only an hour late. It was easy to lose track of time. But what if he was injured?

Fee went into the hut and buttoned on her cargo jacket and strapped on her pistol. She clipped on a first aid kit and water bottle plus her bear spray canister. She slipped her night goggles in her breast pocket, then radioed the emergency number.

"Banff Services Search and Rescue."

"It's Fiona MacRae. I'm at Field Research Outlook blind 14. Dr. Matt Bracken hasn't returned from his night rounds at the expected time. He's over an hour late."

"Fiona, are you requesting a search?"

"No, this is an alert that there may be an emergency. I will search for Matt myself. I'll do a half-mile radius search from Blind 14. He is not responding to his radio."

"Fiona, we don't recommend a single person search. The helicopter was deployed today, flying firefighters to Zone R-2. It's in Calgary but expected back in about 30 minutes. We could have our helicopter to Blind 14 in

about forty-five minutes with more searchers. Then do a flyover with our searchlight and body-heat sensors."

"I'm not waiting. The fire has pushed more large predators into Zone R-1. Matt's likely to be attacked if he is injured."

"We'll be standing by. Please check-in at fifteen-minute intervals with your co-ordinates. I assume that you're armed?"

"I have my pistol and bear spray. Matt has the rifle plus bear spray. I'll begin my search going north for twenty minutes, about half a mile, and change direction every twenty minutes proceeding clockwise."

As Fee crossed the grassland and entered the dense growth of trees, her heart beat faster. She was rushing into an unsafe situation. For good reasons, Little Red Riding Hood was warned not to go into the woods alone.

The shadows were filled with eyes watching her and rustling sounds as if a beast was creeping toward her. When she put on her night goggles, the shadows became light green, and her vision got better. She kept one hand hovering near her pistol. Every couple of minutes, she yelled Matt's name and then listened.

The forest got quieter. Its inhabitants watched her, sensed danger.

She tried calling Matt on the radio one more time. No reply. *Shit! Double shit.* She tripped over a tree root, caught a tree branch, righting herself. A twinge of pain from the muscles around her ribs reminded her she was supposed to be resting them. Not tonight.

She had to find Matt.

Should she look down instead of ahead? If Matt was injured, he might be on the ground, but she wouldn't be any good to him if she were attacked.

After about 20 minutes, she'd traveled about half a mile, so she turned east. She'd checked in with Search and Rescue. They had ordered air support to return to Banff. They could deploy to Blind 14 in about 35 minutes.

Fee blew her whistle now because she was going hoarse from shouting. Her radio crackled to life.

"Fiona, Matt checked in with us. His radio was damaged in a fall. Nothing serious, a twisted ankle. He's at the blind on the back-up radio and wants your co-ordinates. Call him at 6710. Confirm this message received."

"Message received."

Fee looked around her. Exact coordinates? The trees seemed to move closer. There was barely a thin beam of moonlight filtering through the sooty branches that stretched out like demon wings descending.

She peered at her compass face through her night goggles. She could read the bearings. She called Matt on the new call sign.

"Matt, it's Fee."

"Where the hell are you? You shouldn't be out there alone, goddamn it!"

"I don't think you're supposed to swear on the radio."

"Oh, for God's sake, never mind that. What are your coordinates?"

"Are you planning to come to me? With that twisted ankle?"

"You are bloody right, I am!"

"Then I'm not giving them to you."

The swearing broadcast after that would earn Matt a well-deserved lecture on radio protocol if anyone were monitoring the call.

"I will backtrack the way I came using the coordinates I took. I've walked for about 35 minutes. It will probably take the same time to get back."

A calmer voice came back on the radio to her.

"All right, Fee, I won't come to you, I promise. Please give me the coordinates."

Fee scanned the area. Was she close to a cougar or wolf den? Both hunted at night. She radioed the coordinates.

Matt responded at once. "You're in wolf pack # 6's hunting ground, and two cougars frequent that area. Keep your bear spray handy and move as fast as you can without tripping. I'll get a large campfire going in the clearing. You'll see it once you're going south and the trees thin. Keep your radio on active."

Fee was already on the move. She clutched her canister of bear spray as she blundered through the dense growth, not trying to be quiet. Any predators had smelled her by now. In fact, her noise could prove a deterrent to predators if she were lucky for a change. Her other hand was close to her holster, but she didn't take out her gun because she might fall and shoot herself.

No need to panic. You've been in scary places before today. Keep up your speed. Fee's inner voice calmed her, willing her to breathe slower and deeper, to be vigilant. She hadn't looked up to check for a cougar ready to pounce because she'd been bolting down the path.

Closer than she liked, she heard a wolf howl. It was her turn to swear. When she reached the coordinates, she changed direction.

"Heading south toward the blind." She gave her coordinates.

"You should see the campfire in about 15 minutes. You're making good time."

Branches slapped her in the face, and cobwebs were dangling from her hair and sticking to her as she blundered up the path. She brushed them away and kept going. At last, she could see the light from the campfire glowing small in the distance. Her heart leaped and then froze. Blocking her pathway was a hulking, silver wolf, teeth bared.

Fee shouted into her radio, "Wolf!"

She drew her pistol and kept watching it without making eye contact. She screamed as loud and as aggressively as she could, "Get away! Get out of here!" She edged to a tree. The wolf moved closer. She fired at his shoulder and heard a yowl of pain as it swung around and disappeared. Fee scrambled up the tree.

"I wounded the wolf on his shoulder. He's taken off. I'm about ten feet up a tree, right next to the trail, about fifteen minutes away from you."

"I'm on my way. Stay there. It will take me more time with this blasted ankle."

"Don't come. If you're limping, the wolf will see you as easy prey. I can wait until it's light at dawn, then I'll walk the rest of the way. The wounded wolf should be gone by then."

"I'm coming NOW."

No point arguing.

"I'll blow my whistle to help guide you." She blew a loud blast, then she shifted her night goggles and surveyed the tree. She hadn't checked for cougars in her mad clamber up it. Apart from the tree's small nightly inhabitants like possums and owls who were blinking tiny astonished eyes at her, she appeared to be alone. Luck at last.

"Can you hear my whistle?"

"Yes, you're on the trail, no problem finding you, but the whistle will tell me what tree you're up."

She peered down, seeking a sign of the wolf. He was like a ghost with that gray coat. She hadn't aimed to kill him, just to graze him. Now wounded, the wolf would be even more aggressive, but Fee had to buy time to get up the tree.

If the wolf were still around, Matt was in danger of attack. The stubborn damn man should have listened to her and waited until daylight.

She sighted her pistol on the trail and prepared to shoot to kill.

"Matt, I can see you!" She blew her whistle and waved. Matt looked up just as a smoky shape leaped from the trees at him. Frantic, Fee tried to separate the wolf from him as she aimed her pistol. There was no clear shot.

Suddenly the wolf collapsed, coughing and choking. Matt had managed to bear spray it. Now he blindly stumbled away, obviously holding his breath to avoid the fumes. Fee scrambled down the tree to Matt's side, grabbed him, and dragged him past the wolf, down the track.

"Let's get the hell out of here! We have ten minutes max."

Fee crashed ahead while Matt stumbled along behind her. When she reached the field, she bolted to the fire, grabbed two burning sticks, and headed back up the trail. Matt was limping worse and had slowed even more. She thrust a fire torch in his hand and walked backward behind him, holding her own firestick in one hand and her pistol in the other. No sign of the wolf yet.

They broke into the clearing and made for the stairs of the blind. A pack of wolves, running silent, entered the meadow about twenty feet away, slowing at the sight of the blazing fire. Matt turned on them, dropped his torch, fired a rifle shot, kicking up the dirt in front of them. The wolves stopped and stared. Yellow eyes assessed the fleeing prey.

Matt and Fee made it to the blind scarcely before the pack came after them.

"Fee, climb the stairs and give me cover!"

Fee scrambled up the rope stairs, turned, and fired over Matt's head as he pulled himself up, dragging one foot.

Her warning bullets whistled close to the running wolves, but they kept coming. Her next shot ripped through the lead wolf's ear. He yelped and swerved toward the trees. The pack followed.

Matt hauled the stairs up and secured them, far above any further threats. They both sank down on the bench facing the campfire in the empty space.

Matt turned toward Fee, opened his mouth to speak, and stopped. The moonlight reflected tears on her cheeks as she leaned her head on his shoulder, letting out a huge breath. He reached his arm around her slender shoulders and drew her close. Tomorrow they would discuss her insane behavior. Tonight wasn't the time.

Chapter 12

The sun was too bright. Matt opened his eyes and groaned. It had to be around 7:00 a.m. He turned toward Fee. Not there. Matt swore, which was becoming a habit around her. Could she, for once, be where she was supposed to be —snuggled up to him, warm and safe in bed?

Last night, he'd woken up three times to check on her. His psyche wasn't over his panic attack when he'd realized Fee was out searching for him — alone. A wave of relief washed over him when, each time, he saw her sleeping face. Her forehead had a red scratch above the right eyebrow, and her hair was full of cobwebs.

Earlier, Fee had insisted that he soak his ankle in cool water to reduce the swelling while she made up the bed.

Next, she ordered him to sit still while she bound the ankle in a supporting, elastic bandage from the first aid kit, followed by a demand that he swallows an anti-inflammatory pain killer too.

After being commanded to get into bed, he couldn't resist rebelling a bit. He propped himself with the chair back while he stripped off his cargo pants and jacket and shirt, then grabbed his waistband and peeled off his underwear. Upright, he stretched and yawned, raising his brawny arms, causing a tidal wave of muscles to ripple up his torso to a brazen grin full of shameful invitation. Fee's gasp was his applause for the strip show.

Her reckless behavior still disturbed him, but this afternoon's sexual delights were also still fresh in his mind, which voted for an encore. He made himself comfortable in the bed.

Fee drank a glass of water and tried to decide what to do next. Funny how fleeing from wolves had taken her mind off the day's other events, but Matt had somehow managed to stay focused. He had her attention, no small feat with her being 'bootlicking' tired. His body was magnificent human male that deserved a charcoal sketch just like this, naked. But right now, sketching him using Braille flitted into her mind.

She unlaced her boots, stripped off everything but her bra and underwear. Matt was watching, and with all her heart, she wished she had even a shot glass of energy left.

Fee blew out the candle, reached behind and unhooked her bra, freeing her breasts, and then shucked her underwear. After the hot sex this afternoon, she could hardly go back to sleeping with him in a T-shirt and underwear.

As she climbed onto the bed, Matt pulled her toward him, engulfing her shapely, nude body in his arms. His rock-hard manhood touched her, demanding.

"Matt, I'm wiped out. Do you think — later?"

"Rest, Fee. Stop thinking. I'll stand down my weapon." He kissed her neck.

Matt read her well. For a moment tonight, she had thought he was angry with her, but likely it was merely stress she saw in his face. Matt rubbed her back, and she was asleep in minutes.

Two hours later, Matt awoke as he realized Fee was stroking him. Still asleep, she was running her fingers over his thighs and buttocks, as if sketching his outline. Her velvet fingertips traced a tingling path, defining each muscle. His breathing rocketed as her fingers reached his manhood, and began stroking his shaft and encircling the head. As he hardened, she pulled herself up over him, spread her legs to envelope him inside her silky wet cleft, moving on him in a rhythm of sheer sensual delight. Matt held onto her hips and joined the dance.

As they reached their breathless pinnacle, Fee sighed and fell onto his chest, still asleep, nuzzling her cheek into the dark curls by his throat. Matt kissed her head, reflecting that she was the wildest and most endearing nymph he had ever taken into his bed.

—*—

Where was she right now? Last night when he had twisted his ankle, he had been on his way back to warn her to be extra cautious because he had spotted a new pack of wolves fleeing from the fire. They were now vying for dominance with wolf pack #6. The wolves were fighting a turf war, judging from the blood and tufts of wolf fur left behind. They were trying to lay claim to the prey in this territory, and a small human stumbling around in the dark met the criteria.

He broke into an anxiety sweat afresh.

"Here's breakfast, sleepyhead." The door creaked open, and Fee poked her head into the room, then marched in with a large trout dripping water on the floor, and her fishing gear in her other hand. A bear spray canister was clipped to her waist.

"I didn't clean it down by the river this time. I'll do that on the deck here to not attract last night's unwanted visitors."

Her brave smile didn't fool him. He had a good idea of the courage it took to go out in the pale early morning light after last night, cross the grass to the river and fish alone. It was also foolish beyond words.

He swore.

"Didn't last night's experience teach you anything?"

Fee stared at him, her smile faded, and her eyes clouded. "Well, that is a nice attitude from someone whose life I saved. I take it you don't do gratitude?" She turned on her heel and stomped out to the deck to clean the fish.

Matt swung his legs out of bed, grimacing when he forgot his injury, putting weight on his foot with the swollen ankle. He swore so much he sounded like he was praying.

Why hadn't he explained the real situation to her last night? Chiefly, because he could see that she was drained from the whole nightmare of it. He wanted her to sleep, to be rested in the morning so they could have a sensible discussion during which he would point out her errors in judgment.

He hadn't expected her to rise at dawn and go fishing by herself with at least one aggressive wolf pack nearby.

He struggled into pants, and his last clean white T-shirt. He had better give her the facts of their situation fast before she got herself killed. He hobbled out to the deck.

Fee had finished cleaning the trout with rare brutality, tearing the innards out, and sealing them in a plastic bag. Finally, her breathing slowed, calming her.

Matt hobbled out, grabbing the hut wall for support, then scowled at her.

"Jeez, you look like someone spit in your coffee. What's the matter? Is your ankle terrible?" Fee scrutinized his face.

"Fee, we must talk right now about safety protocols. You're lucky that we aren't airlifting your half-eaten, mangled body out of here after last night's irrational actions—and this morning's too." Matt's face was grim at the horrific image.

"What are you talking about? I followed safety protocols to the letter, and you know it!"

Fee flung the fish down and marched back into the hut. There was no satisfying him. He put her in the wrong no matter what she did. She'd followed safety protocols, and saved the damn man's life! She didn't need the aggravation. Likely she could hitch a ride on one of the Search and Rescue helicopters flying back and forth to the fire.

"What are you doing? We haven't discussed anything yet."

Matt stood leaning on the doorframe, observing the whirling dervish shoving things into her backpack. Fee's gray eyes were thunder clouds.

"There's nothing to discuss. You're determined to criticize me no matter what and to be an ungrateful jerk while you're doing it. I'm out of here as fast as I can arrange transportation."

"Look, we have to talk, if only for your safety until you leave. Will you please stop for a few minutes and hear me out?"

Fee stopped packing, grabbed his boots, aimed, and fired, hitting him in the stomach — twice. As she reached for her water bottle, Matt snatched his radio and left, slamming the hut door as the metal bottle thudded into it.

That was it. What planet had he been on? This was Fiona MacRae, the most obstinate woman he had ever rashly taken to bed. He would not waste more time trying to reason with her.

How did he get into this mess? Poor, bloody judgment, that's how — unable to resist the chance of sizzling sex. In his defense, no man could have refused Fee's seriously hot wake-up call last night.

Even though his ankle injury prevented him from working, he had planned on giving Fee a few more days at the blind to finish her work. But now things were complicated by too much drama.

Aside from his ankle needing a week to recover, not the best shape to be in the wilderness, he would have to deal with a furious hellcat at the same time. He radioed Search and Rescue for a pick-up.

"Can you be ready in two hours? We have a re-supply flight returning to base, passing over Outlook Blind #14 about then."

"Yes, no problem. We'll be ready."

They finished packing up in record time, passing a few stilted comments as they worked together, lugging equipment down the steps. No conversation was possible in the noisy helicopter, and radio chatter filled the jeep on the ride back to Zone R-1.

The Aid Station supplied Matt with ice packs and anti-inflammatory tablets for his ankle. It turned out that his ankle was strained ligaments that needed ice, elevation, and rest — no fleeing through the woods for a minimum of a week.

A volunteer agreed to help them back to their cabins. When they reached Fee's, there was an awkward moment when the volunteer asked Fee if she'd check daily on Matt while he was healing?

Fee agreed, waved them off, then turned and climbed the steps to her cabin. She closed the door, shrugged off her pack, sank down on the bed and stared at the floor.

Chapter 13

Matt unpacked his gear, depositing his dirty clothes in a heap to be soaked and washed. He should ice his ankle, but he felt like he was waiting for something. It was strange how quiet the cabin seemed. Even weirder was how he hadn't minded Fee bustling around him, although he usually preferred to be alone while working.

She was always busy, always saying something funny. The times she was quiet was when she was in observation mode, or when she focused on her sketching. Her smoky eyes would hardly blink as she captured precisely the right angle of a badger's elongated head or the tufts of hair on the asymmetrical ears of an owl.

He reached into the bottom of his backpack, searching for a missing sock and pulled out the zip lock bag of trout fillets Fee had cleaned that morning.

Well, shit! Now he felt guilty for being gruff with her when she'd made such a brave effort to get breakfast for them. He could see her cute face grinning as she displayed her catch. When had she slipped the fillets into his bag?

Yeah, he could have been more sensitive, but she was totally unreasonable in her reaction. He wasn't criticizing her. He wanted to keep her safe, to protect her.

And that was the problem. He was too protective of Fee, almost had a heart attack when he realized she was in a life-threatening situation because of him. How could he face all that beauty and spirit destroyed by a ravaging wolf's teeth? They were both better off now that they ended the field trip.

They could back to getting their work done with no further complications, rarely encountering each other. Besides, Fee made it clear that's exactly what she wants.

He hobbled to the fridge, tossed the trout into the freezer, slamming the door. It was hard to avoid thinking about what he was missing, such as Fee's laughter and fierce caring that made her put herself in grave danger to save him — not to mention her luscious body, slick with the heat of her sex as she enfolded him, and her eagerness for life's sensuous pleasures. Matt swore — his new pastime.

—*—

Fee finished unpacking and then organized her sketches and digital photos. She had checked off her list several animals and plants in a short time, but some, like cougars, would be hard to get now that she was far from their habitat.

Perched on her top step, Fee ate a bowl of chicken soup and gazed up at the stars. It was a cloudless night, quiet with no wolf howls.

Well, hell. Her pride had cost her a professional opportunity she needed and, personally, the hottest sex she'd ever had with a man — a man she respected and liked when she wasn't overreacting. It had felt awesome to be on the receiving end of his tender care and bone-melting sex — but not as great a feeling receiving his sarcasm and anger.

Her wounded pride and fiery temper had got the best of her. Her decision to return to her cabin was impulsive, so it shocked her when Matt acted on it right away. No time for her to calm down and change her mind. That must have been what he wanted. It was no more than sex for him, a fling, and when he didn't like her behavior, he put an end to it.

She didn't realize that flings allowed no differences of opinion. Another fling rule he hadn't revealed. The next time she'd be wiser, choose better — if she had another one.

Unbidden, an image formed of Matt's raven hair and brawny shoulders as he kneeled before her, opening her sex with his lips and invading tongue. She could feel his forehead resting on her pelvic bone, his hot hands stroking her butt cheeks, a finger sliding down between them. As she moistened, she shifted her knees apart. Whoa! This replay of Matt's sexual lure and tender care was firing her libido. Next fling? The sooner, the better.

—*—

The radio call to Matt was brief.

"I'm fine, Fee. The swelling is almost gone."

"Do you need anything?"

"I've run out of coffee, but it's no problem. You don't have to bring any. I can tough out the caffeine withdrawal for a few more days."

"I'll be close to your cabin this evening. Geoff spotted a pine marten den near you. I will get photos of the family when they come out of their den to hunt tonight. I'll drop by coffee beans when I finish."

"Geoff?"

"Geoff Halloran. You remember, the conservation officer. He stopped by yesterday. Didn't you see him?"

"No, I guess I wasn't on his visitation list."

"Oh. Well, I better get going. See you later."

Matt sat choking the radio in his clenched hand. He wasn't surprised that Geoff was sniffing around Fee, given his reaction to her at the Outlook blind. She'd be a compelling draw for any straight guy plus Geoff had seen her braless in a wet T-shirt, her cheeks flushed from red hot sex, her flame hair wild, and her big eyes reflecting pure arousal.

Matt felt himself harden, and without thinking, began to stroke his shaft. Son of a bitch, he should forget her now that he had made the break.

Instead, he dreamed of Fee, often waking up harder than a sledgehammer. Worse, her scent wafted off the cargo shirt he had lent her. He was about to wash it, but instead, he buried his face in the cotton fabric, fantasizing about stripping her, inhaling her scent, tasting her private, feminine spots. What the hell!

Judging by her tone on the radio, Fee didn't have a problem of cooling down her ardor. Did she realize that Geoff had an ulterior motive for being unusually helpful? Maybe she even welcomed his intentions?

Matt knew he had talked Fee into a fling and then had broken it off after two days. Was she opposed to flings now? Or perhaps he had awakened her passionate, lustful nature, and she needed to satisfy it?

His swearing frightened a woodchuck who was hanging around his small garden patch of onions and carrots.

An hour before twilight, Fee tiptoed to a concealed observation spot upwind from the den, hidden in a hollow under an ancient pine's exposed root. This spring's litter, close to maturity, would be the size of small cats, crowding the den. Like most predators, the pine martens liked to hunt at night. Fee hoped to record one as it leaped from tree to tree in a moonlight pursuit of small prey.

Tonight, her mind was as busy as a pine marten as it chased thoughts of Matt. He would survive without the coffee, but it was an excuse for her to come by Matt's cabin. Since the Outlook blind, they had spoken on the radio, but never in person.

Why did she have a yen to see him? The man she'd sworn off, who had returned the favor and dropped her as fast as he could? No regretful goodbye from Matt, nothing but a silent packing up and getting her out of his space. Two days of enjoying her intimate favors were more than enough for him. Why was she surprised? He had put a time limit of a week on the fling.

Was it a mere matter of the scorching sex for her too? Or was it the memory of being held against his sheltering chest when he carried her? Or his gentle kiss to comfort and reassure her? What difference did it make? The fling was over and, according to the rules, she should just be getting on with her life as if "as if nothing had happened."

It didn't feel over if her dreams of Matt meant

anything. Neither did it seem ended when she remembered his sheer masculine scent, the silken texture of his chest hair, or his deep golden, penetrating gaze as they reached the heights of mutual pleasure and climaxed together.

Nope, she was failing at the "fling game." She couldn't convince her heart or body that nothing had happened. They weren't buying it.

She better skip seeing Matt tonight. In this state of mind, she might throw down the coffee beans and climb him like a tree.

Matt was watching for Fee as it had been dark for an hour. She should be here by now. He had showered and put on clean jeans and a buttery yellow cotton shirt. He was also clean-shaven. *Are you getting ready for a hot date? Keep in mind you're not — absolutely not — going to touch Fee tonight, not even shake hands, got it? It's over.*

He heard a rustling outside the cabin door, swung it open in time to see Fee turn, and rush away.

"Fee, wait!" As he stepped toward her, he tripped over a small bag of coffee beans, wrenching his sore ankle. He swore and gripped the doorframe.

"Were you trying to injure me, setting a tripping hazard?" He couldn't see her face in the black night. The moon was hiding behind threatening clouds.

"I didn't want to bother you this late — and I'd appreciate it if you didn't swear at me." Fee ambled back to his door. So much for a fast getaway.

Matt smiled when he heard her 'take no crap' voice. "Sorry. I've developed a cussing habit recently. It's not late for me. Why don't you come in for a few minutes? I've brewed lemon mint tea."

"Thanks, but by the look of those clouds, I'll be lucky to get to my cabin before it rains."

She couldn't see Matt, but hearing his deep inviting voice was causing her heartbeat to do a happy dance. She'd better get going — now.

Matt checked the darkening sky. He shouldn't delay Fee, but what if the storm hit and she had to spend the night?

"I found a camera lens of yours in my backpack, and a weird metal thing. Come in and get them, then you can go."

Fee slipped off her small pack. Matt bent over and picked up the bag of coffee beans as Fee moved toward the cabin door. She stumbled into him, and his arms went around her, steadying. Swirling clouds rolled away, the moonlight revealing Fee's face filled with naked hunger, and Matt answered with his own hunger, claiming her lips in a crushing kiss.

Fee felt herself sink into his heat, his intoxicating clean scent of pine and soap, his hard chest, his mighty arms, his demanding lips, and — a world of hurt. Fee shoved him away.

"You can't do this. Stop teasing me. Stay away from me!" She grabbed her backpack, turned, and rushed up the path into the forest. When she was well out of sight, she stopped, dug out her night headlight, put on her rain slicker, and brushed the tears from her face. Soon a downpour pounded her all the way home.

Tucked into her small bed, listening to the rain beating on her window, it was a poor comfort believing she'd done the right thing. There was no point in sharing a passion with a man who had no feelings for her. Her body didn't agree, but she punched her pillow, turned over, and refused to listen.

Matt sat by the fire, his legs stretched out, his mint tea laced with two fingers of whiskey. Fee didn't trust him anymore — and she wasn't wrong. He couldn't even trust himself to play fair around her. He could still feel her breasts pushed against his chest, her upturned face filled with need, and her bewitching mouth welcoming him. How could he resist? Her eyes revealed her lack of artifice. She couldn't play the game, and worse, he was breaking the rules himself.

Tossing back the whiskey, he made the decision to return to Blind #14, catch up on work and forget about Fee. He wondered which determined wolf pack had won

the territorial war. He'd lost his battle with one small red-
headed foxy gal — time to retreat.

Chapter 14

The rain kept right on pounding down the next few days. Fee sat on the porch in a well-worn oversized sweater working on her pine marten sketches, grateful for the cabin's overhang that allowed her to work outdoors. Her potbelly stove's heat was keeping the cabin toasty, and a coffee pot perked away on it.

"I thought you would be inside today, keeping warm and dry."

Fee looked up to see the tall figure of Geoff Halloran wearing a dripping yellow rain slicker with the hood up. His bright blue eyes sparkled as his broad smile beamed at her.

"I'm a nature girl who would rather be outside, rain or shine. I was about to take a break. Come inside if you have time, and I'll pour you a hot coffee. I can rustle up ginger cookies, hardly stale."

"How can I refuse such an offer?" Geoff followed her inside but then stepped back outside to take off his dripping slicker and hang it on a hook outside by the door. The cabin sure didn't have much room for maneuvering.

Fee pulled off her heavy sweater, tossed it on the bed, revealing underneath a peach T-shirt tucked into her form-fitting blue jeans.

Geoff's grin got even broader if possible, as he admired her shapely trim body.

Fee poured the coffee, handed him a mug, and snagged the bag of cookies off a shelf.

"What are you doing out in the rain yourself?"

"I've come with an offer for you for Saturday if you don't have other plans. How about a day trip to observe a family of cougars in Zone 3?"

"Sure, I'd love it, but what do you mean 'observe them'? Cougars aren't likely to tolerate our presence. They'll be gone as soon as they see us, or even attack us. And observing them from a tree isn't an option."

Geoff smiled at Fee in genuine admiration. He liked how she was no amateur when it came to animal behavior.

"They're in captivity at the moment. The mother has burns from the fire. She was tranquilized and then moved with her cubs to the animal rehab center in Zone 3. It's not perfect, but it is a chance to see them up close.

They're doing so well they're being released back in Zone R-2 early next week."

"Then you've got a deal! If you don't mind giving up your day off?"

"This will be a pleasure, not work. I thought we might have a swim and a picnic at a waterfall near to the rehab center." Geoff gauged her reaction. He wasn't sure if she was involved with someone — in particular, Dr. Matt Bracken.

Fiona beamed at him, "I'd enjoy that. What time should we meet on Saturday?" Geoff skimmed his fingers over her hand as she passed the cookies to him. God, she was even more stunning when she smiled.

Matt was passing by Fiona's cabin. Now that his ankle was healed, he'd been to the town of Banff for extra supplies for his return to Zone R-2. He spotted Geoff's rain slicker hanging by her door, heard Geoff's deep voice rumbled from inside her cabin.

This was an excellent time to tell Fee he'd be away next week. Matt's mind called *bullshit*, but he ignored it.

As Geoff came out on to the porch with Fee, Matt stepped behind a clump of trees.

"Great, I'll pick you up at 9:00 a.m. Saturday. Don't forget your bathing suit. I'll have a surprise for you in the picnic basket, so don't bring any food." He wrestled into his rain slicker and leaned over Fee.

Matt couldn't tell if Geoff was kissing her because the damn slicker was in the way. Shortly Geoff strode off up the trail, passing within a few feet of Matt who was camouflaged in his olive green raincoat. Matt thought he heard Geoff whistling.

Fee stood on the porch, lost in thought. Finally, she was going to study cougars in action, plus, she had a date for Saturday with a damn good looking guy. Geoff was interested, and she sure needed a distraction. She didn't want to spend the rest of her summer yearning after Matt, who didn't want her. What famous movie star said, "The cure for one man was the next one"?

"Hello, Fee," Matt said.

Fee jumped, then crossed her arms and glared at him. Why did Matt have to show up just when she was conjuring a fantasy about Geoff? It was as if she had summoned Matt instead in all his masculine glory, raindrops on his lashes, his golden-brown eyes penetrating hers.

"I've stopped by to tell you that I'll be in Zone R-2 all next week. I won't be available in case of emergency."

"Doesn't your radio work?" She didn't care if she sounded surly.

"Works fine. I'm only here in person to replace the coffee you lent me. Can I open my pack on your porch? I don't want to get my stuff wet."

Fee moved aside, and Matt shrugged off his pack onto the porch, then pulled off his slicker, and hung it up. She watched him shift his mighty shoulders, mesmerized by the tight jeans that stretched over his butt as he kneeled down to sort through the pack. She remembered tracing that curve with her fingers.

"Fee? Fee? What's on your mind, or should I say 'Who'? Was that Geoff Halloran I saw on the trail?" He watched a guilty look flit across her face. Oh, damn. Could she have feelings for Geoff already? He felt a sinking sensation as if he was losing something.

"Oh, sorry, my mind was somewhere else. Yes, Geoff was here. He's taking me to the Zone 3 Animal Rehab on Saturday to sketch a cougar family."

"I thought you wanted to view the animals in their natural habitats?"

"Yes, but I'd have to be back in Zone R-2 for that; therefore, I must make do with this opportunity." Fee narrowed her eyes at him.

"If I remember, you were the one dying to leave. You couldn't pack fast enough."

"Well, I was angry, but I would have gotten over it if you'd given me a chance, but you were in a hurry to get rid of me." Her eyes felt wet. Matt was another man who couldn't wait to abandon her.

They studied each other. Matt could see the tears in Fee's eyes. He'd hurt her. No use denying the charge, he

was guilty, had wanted to escape the drama. What could he say?

"Look, Fee, I was angry too, but now I . . ."

Fee stepped back and held up her hand to stop him speaking. The rejection was painful the first time without going through a repeat of it, even if Matt wasn't angry now.

"No use going over it. It's done. Now, if you'll excuse me, I must get on with my work. I have a lot to get done before Saturday." She turned, walked into the cabin, and slammed the door.

Oh, but now you have the added perk of the attentive Geoff to help you with your work. Matt was tempted to fling open the door, kiss and stroke Fee until she was senseless, driving out any thought of Geoff — but then what? Matt ached to hold her, comfort her, and bury his face in her mess of curls. He hated hurting her, but what could he do now? For sure, she would refuse a proposal of another fling, but he could offer nothing more than that.

Matt put his slicker on, hefted his backpack, putting the coffee in a dry spot near the door. He had three days before her Saturday date to figure out a strategy.

—*—

"So, Sis, how are you faring in the wilds? How did your field trip with 'tall, dark, and wolfish' go?" Duncan's cheery voice was a welcome interruption to Fee's low mood. She'd been second-guessing herself over how she'd handled things with Matt. Should she have heard him out? Her damn temper had once more ruined any chance of her being reasonable.

"We had to cut it short, but I captured quite a few of the animals I needed in the two days we had."

"That's great, but why shorten the time?"

"Matt injured his ankle, and there was a forest fire in the zone next to us." She wasn't lying, merely omitting the real reason for the sudden departure.

"So, when are you going back?"

"Matt's going back next week to Outlook Blind #14, but I'm not."

"Why not?"

"We didn't enjoy each other's company enough to repeat the experience."

"Oh, Fee, I'm sorry, but two days doesn't seem enough time to decide you're incompatible. I mean you both were busy working, so you didn't have much time together. What happened?"

"Dunc, I'm sorry, but I don't want to talk about it. It's finished. The end."

"Sorry, Fee. I didn't mean to pressure you, but I hope you aren't overreacting to a small thing. Your quick temper can get the best of you, which you admit."

"Well, thanks for blaming the failure on me."

After that, Duncan apologized, and the conversation ended with Fee even more miserable. She knew Duncan would worry about her now. She could have confided in him about the situation, but that meant reliving it.

She needed fresh air. The rain had stopped, so she pulled on her sweater and headed out for a walk in nature, always soothing for her heart and soul.

Duncan sat at his desk, thinking about Fee. She had no luck in her relationships. What had happened this time? He hoped that she wasn't letting her temper and pride end what appeared to him to be a promising match. He'd heard more hurt than anger in her voice. It was time for him to pay her a brotherly visit.

Or even better, why not visit Matt? Duncan grimaced. *Brother or not, I better wear inflammable clothes if I'm planning to meddle in Fee's love life.*

Chapter 15

It was near noon the next day, and Matt was about to make lunch when he heard groans like an injured animal nearby. He shouldered his rifle and stepped out the door as Duncan staggered into the clearing.

"Oh, thank God you're here." Duncan was soaked in sweat, his glasses fogged up, and his face beet red. "I took the wrong turn twice. I've been rambling around for hours trying to find you."

"What's happened to Fee?" Matt felt like a giant hand was squeezing his heart.

"Fee? No, no, she's fine. Can I have water?" Duncan looked like he was ready to collapse.

In short order, he was sitting in an armchair sipping frosty lemonade. Matt was across from him, trying to disguise his impatience while he waited for Duncan to recover.

"Duncan, what can I do for you? You didn't come all this way just for exercise."

"You'll want to tell me to mind my business, and you'd be right, but I hope you understand that I've Fee's well-being at heart — and yours too. May I ask a personal question?"

"Well, you've made a huge effort to ask it in person, so go ahead and ask." Matt crossed his arms and kept his face blank.

"Why isn't Fee going back with you next week to the blind?" Duncan gave Matt his most piercing stare, the one that made his student interns shiver.

Matt seemed surprised by the question, then relieved. Duncan suspected that Matt had been expecting a reprimand from an irate brother for seducing his fair sister and then dropping her.

"Duncan, we haven't discussed it. Fee hasn't asked to go back."

"Would you ask her?"

"It's more complicated than that. I doubt Fee would go back to the blind with me."

"Ask her, anyway." Duncan smiled. Matt must still have feelings for Fee, or he would have refused outright.

"Did Fee ask you to talk to me?"

"No, and I'd be grateful if you didn't mention that I was here. I've overstepped the boundaries of a big brother. If possible, I'd like to avoid Fee's fury at my interference."

"I've no objections to Fee going with me to the blind, but I have no idea how to convince her to come. Do you have any suggestions? She can be obstinate."

"It runs in the family." Duncan chuckled. "My advice is to point out the advantages of her going back to the blind for her work. She will find that hard to resist, no matter how annoyed she is with you."

Matt didn't answer. He was rolling the idea over in his mind. Duncan might be matchmaking, but at least one MacRae approved of him.

"All right, I'll ask her tonight, but now, would you like lunch? I'm making canned salmon sandwiches. Are you going to see Fee today?"

"No way! She'd be suspicious about me showing up unexpectedly, and I'm a lousy liar. But would you make sure that I make it to the parking lot without getting lost again? I'd rather not be roadkill on the side of a trail, probably run over by a moose."

—*—

It had been a busy day. Fee sat outside by the fire, sipped a chamomile tea, and dried her shampooed hair.

She was ready for bed, braless, wearing her sleep camisole and shorts. It was one of those balmy summer nights, with scented air and bright stars that fueled the hankering for summer during blustery, frigid prairie winters. She'd been pushing herself to get as much done as possible before the next day when she'd be off to Zone 3 with Geoff.

Many of her target animals hibernated in the winter. For the tenth time, Fee wished she'd been able to stay more than a few days in the Outlook Blind #14 area. She needed to go back, but from her experience so far, she knew going alone wasn't a smart idea. If things went well with Geoff on Saturday, she could ask him to go on a field trip with her. But did she want to get that personal with Geoff?

It was no secret to her *whom* she truly wanted to be 'up close and personal with,' but she wasn't going to think about Matt. It was bad enough that he visited her at night in her dreams. Her psyche was enjoying itself repeating the most torrid scenes in full color, adding bawdy twists. And she was missing his cheeky grin, his sweet concern, his understanding of her passion for all of God's creatures.

"May I share your fire?"

Startled, Fee splashed her hot tea, narrowly missing her bare leg.

"Do you have to sneak up on me? I almost scalded myself!"

"Sorry, I thought you saw me. I guess you were too far away in thought. Next time I'll whistle when I'm approaching you." Matt pursed his lips and began whistling an old Scottish tune, then switched to a song. He sounded like a bull calf was standing on his windpipe. He stopped when Fee started to laugh.

"Fine, that will work. Don't strain yourself." She couldn't help smiling up at him, her face lit by the firelight.

Matt sat down on the log close enough to enjoy the flowery scent of her damp hair. He longed to nuzzle her neck, filling his senses with her femininity. That camisole was hiding nothing either. He tried not to stare.

"Apart from prowling around, startling unwary fire gazers, what are you doing here?" Matt's proximity had the usual effect on her breathing, plus he regarded her like he was a cougar about to spring.

"I want to talk to you about next week."

"You're going back to Outlook Blind #14. You told me. Do you need me to check on your garden patch?" Fee kept her voice neutral.

"No, but thanks. It's nice of you to offer, but that isn't what I wanted to ask you." He had one chance to get this right — better use his best argument upfront.

"You didn't finish your work at the blind, Fee, but going back there by yourself is a bad idea."

"I've been thinking about that. I might ask Geoff to go there with me."

"I wasn't aware your friendship with Geoff had progressed to where you'd be willing to go overnight into the field with him. The fling rules in effect?"

"Maybe. What business is it of yours, anyway?" Fee glanced away. She would not admit her true feelings to Matt. Let him think whatever he wanted. Fee sat, awaiting his answer.

Matt scowled and didn't reply. If he didn't get a grip on his jealous reaction, he would blow his chance. He took a deep, slow breath. "I'm sorry. It's not my concern what your relationship is with Geoff. That's your business. I was surprised, that's all. I came by to ask you if you wanted to return to Outlook Blind #14 next week with me on a strictly professional basis.

"Oh, I didn't think you wanted me anywhere near the blind?"

"I've thought about this. Your dedication and talent deserve the chance to complete your project as planned. I don't want to be the reason you can't."

He sounded so sincere that Fee was torn with indecision. She stared at the fire, her mind whirling. Damn! This was precisely what she needed right now for her work, but could she accept an offer this dangerous for her sore heart?

"To be precise, what do you mean by 'strictly professional'?"

"We behave like rational professionals involved in our work. Polite and co-operative with each other, nothing else."

"Where would I sleep?"

"I'll bring an air mattress for the floor for myself. You can have the bed."

Fee wondered why he was this accommodating. Her suspicious mind tried to find a reason to refuse, but couldn't come up with one.

"I'll take the floor. It makes sense because I only need a small air mattress, light to pack in."

"Does this mean you accept my offer?" Matt struggled to keep the pleasure out of his voice.

"Yes, it does — on one condition. You keep your promise to be purely professional."

"I will as long as you are — so no problem at all." He smiled at her and stood up, stretched, flexed his back, and rolled his broad shoulders.

Fee stared. Even in the firelight, Matt was worth observing, but what did he mean *if she* was professional?

"I better get going, it's late, and you have an early morning date with Geoff."

"It's not a date . . . Oh, never mind. What time will we start out on Monday?"

"5:30 am like last time. I'll inform Forestry Services that you'll be with me."

As Matt hiked back to his cabin, he felt triumphant, as if a battle had been won. Why was he elated that Fee was going with him? With her fiery nature and stubbornness, she'd be trouble — he could count on it. Matt kept right on grinning.

Chapter 16

Well, she had done it now. Put herself right back in the lion's den. Fee sat on the curb in the parking lot, waiting for Geoff to arrive. She was far too early because she'd hiked there at breakneck speed, chased by her anxiety about returning to the blind with Matt.

All it took was sitting close to Matt last night to re-ignite her passion for him. Her reactions were anything but professional around him. She was also pleased by his sincere praise for her art and dedication. Matt was too brutally honest to try to flatter her.

"If you don't move, a sparrow might nest in your hair. You look like the statue of *The Thinker*."

Fee hadn't even heard Geoff arrive. He was even more enticing out of his uniform, dressed in hiking boots, tight jeans, and a black T-shirt that clung to his broad shoulders and bulging biceps. His surfer gold streaked hair caught the sun, an errant wave fell down his forehead to startling azure blue eyes. Those eyes were alert and full of good humor.

"Usually, it's bats at night that have that idea about my hair." Fee smiled up at him. "I hope you don't mind, but I have a backpack of equipment with me and a bag for my bathing suit and towel."

"No problem, there's lots of room in the jeep. Hop in, I'll stow your stuff in the back."

The jeep roared as they bounced, dodging the potholes on the road and stirring up the gravel. Fee's hair flew out behind her in bright copper ribbons as the wind whipped her face. She laughed like a teenager on a joyride.

Geoff glanced at her and grinned. Nothing was better than hitting the road for an adventure with a beautiful gal full of fun. He hoped that Fee also enjoyed his company, didn't only see today as an opportunity to sketch the cougars.

Outside the large cat compound wire fence, Fee removed her equipment, set up her tripod, and attached her camera. Geoff arranged the camp chairs. The mother cougar was hyper-alert, standing in front of her two kittens, a low growl behind bared teeth directed at them. Bald spots marred her golden coat, the fur burned off by the forest fire. Both kittens sported bald spots too, and one was missing a small ear.

First, Fee worked with charcoal, glancing, never making eye contact with the mother cougar. On her pad, the family appeared almost by magic. Geoff watched her draw, amazed at how the sketch captured the big cat's fear through small details like the angle of her tail. Fee was a talented artist.

An hour later, the mother had relaxed enough to allow her cubs to suckle as she stretched out under a tree. Fee continued to sketch, smiling to herself as she saw Geoff nod off in the sunshine, slumped in the chair that was too small for him.

Finally, Fee stretched her legs, stood up, and focused the camera. The large cougar twitched her ears, slid her eyes to watch her but did not move. Before long, Fee was snapping away, ignored.

"Are you almost finished?" Geoff whispered.

"Yes, I am. I won't see hunting behavior or a cougar climbing a tree or leaping under these conditions. I must get that when I return to the Outlook blind next week."

Geoff frowned at learning she was returning to the blind but didn't comment.

The road, lined by old-growth trees, was in even worse shape than the one on the way to the rescue compound, and suddenly quit altogether.

"We carry our stuff from here to that hill, but the waterfall isn't far, about 600 yards up the path. You lead, and I'll follow. The path is rocky and slippery." He slung on a large backpack.

Fee had her string bag stuffed with her bathing suit and towel. She'd locked her equipment in the jeep's trunk. Hot from sitting in the sun for hours, she was craving a refreshing swim.

Massive trees leaned over the rocky path, shading it. The branches stretched out to grip Fee's hair, forcing her to stuff it all under her hat. Several times as she slipped on a mossy rock, Geoff reached out, steadying her with a firm hand on her back.

Now they heard the roar of rushing water. The trees gave way to a sunlit, flat landing with a rock overhang like a built-in sun umbrella providing shade. About fifteen feet away, a frothy cascade of water poured over the shelf plunging into a glimmering, green pool, deep and transparent, surrounded by feathery ferns and wildflowers. Fee dropped her bag and stared.

"Wow. It's dazzling." She turned to Geoff beaming. He placed a hand on her shoulder.

"I'm surrounded by beauty." He leaned down and brushed her lips with his. Before she could react, he moved away and began unpacking his bag.

"Let's get our bathing suits on and cool off. I'll change here. You can use the brush down the trail." He pulled his swim shorts out of his bag and stripped off his T-shirt, exposing his chiseled chest and flat gut as he pulled it over his head.

Fee grabbed her bag and retreated to where she couldn't see the finale of Geoff's strip show. Plainly, more was on the menu than a picnic and swim. A single guy and gal in the woods and nothing to prevent Mother Nature taking over — just like Matt and her at the blind. Matt! A wave of guilt swept through her, then anger. Why should she feel guilty? She was free to do whatever with whoever she wanted.

"All right down there?"

"Yep, be there in a minute." Fee scrambled into her emerald green bathing suit, a daring scoop neck one-piece with a high cut leg. Because of its design, she rarely wore it, making it in much better shape than her favorite yellow one. This suit looked like an invitation she wasn't sure she wanted to send to Geoff. She wrapped her beach towel around herself and walked back up to the clearing.

"I was about to check to see if a bear was nibbling on you and . . ." Geoff stopped speaking as Fee dropped her towel. The neckline of emerald silk plunged to her navel, slightly covering half of each breast. Her loose hair flamed in the sun trailing in tendrils down her back as she walked past him to the waterfall, her bottom-cheeks, pale half-moons, winked at him while her shapely tanned thighs and legs flexed like a dancer as she walked.

Geoff followed her, hoping she wouldn't look back. By the tightness felt in his groin, his physical response to her was unmistakable. He needed to chill fast.

Fee picked up speed as she neared the pool, dove into the middle, surfaced under the waterfall and climbed out onto the rock shelf. She laughed, invigorated by the water pouring over her. She pulled her dripping hair into a makeshift ponytail. Geoff grinned at her pleasure as he swam up then vaulted up beside her, his muscled wet body glistened like the oiled torso of a bodybuilder.

"I'm going under to check out flora and fauna. I can stay under for almost three minutes. Don't panic if I don't surface before then."

"No longer, or I will have the pleasure of rescuing you." He grinned his blue eyes gleamed with anticipation.

Fee slipped off the rock shelf like a seal returning home to the sea. The green depths were lit by the sun as she swam close to the underside of the banks where creatures were hiding. She hoped she might spot the pinched face of a river muskrat glaring out at her, or a timid, harmless water snake slithering back to the shadows.

When she surfaced, Geoff was close by. He'd kept track of her movements. "Ready for lunch? I'm hungry."

"Sure. Now that you mention it, I'm starving!" She followed Geoff out of the pool. When they reached the clearing, he grabbed her towel and wrapped it around her, and began to dry her back.

"Hey, that's okay, Geoff. Why don't you rustle up lunch while I dry off and change?" She stepped away from him, picked up her bag, and started for the trail.

"You're not swimming after lunch?" His disappointment was evident in his face.

"Oh, I don't think I'll have time. I can always change back. It's nicer to be dry." No way was she lounging on a blanket in *that* bathing suit with Geoff. She scooted down the path, and when she returned, she was back in her shorts and top with her wet suit hanging over her arm.

Geoff had changed into his jeans and shirt too. He spread out a blanket in the overhang's shade, his wet bathing lay nearby on the rocks drying.

"Put your suit on the rocks and come enjoy my humble feast."

The blanket was heaped with containers of fried chicken, coleslaw, butter rolls, and dill pickles. With a flourish, he pulled out of his pack a chilled bottle of white wine, glasses, a wedge of cheddar cheese, and to top it all off, fresh strawberries and cream.

"Where are the grapes?"

Fee giggled at Geoff's confused expression. "Geoff, I'm impressed. In my neighborhood, this is a gourmet feast. I exist on canned and freeze-dried food most of the time. Thank you."

She sat down, and tackled her plate, relishing the yummy food, the moist saturated air, and the rainbows shimmering in the water spray. Finished eating, she inhaled deeply as Geoff passed her a glass of icy wine. As she sipped it, the tart citrus flavor teased her tongue.

"This spot is paradise." She closed her eyes and felt the light pressure of Geoff's lips as he kissed the top of her nose. Her eyes flew open as his lips found her mouth, and his strong hands gripped her shoulders, pulling her into him.

When Fee didn't respond, Geoff drew back, his blue eyes troubled. "Have I made a mistake? Am I moving too fast for you, Fee?"

"Geoff, I recently ended a *thing* with someone. I guess I'm not ready to get involved yet."

"If you're not ready, I can wait. I don't want to pressure you. We can take it slow — unless you have no interest in me at all?"

"I like you, Geoff, but I'm not over someone, can't move on yet." Her heart sank as she faced the truth about her feelings for Matt. Why had she agreed to return to the blind with him? She must love torture.

Geoff figured he knew who the "someone" was. His competition was likely Dr. Matt Bracken. Given Matt's reputation as a commitment-phobic guy, Geoff guessed Matt hadn't wanted a serious relationship with Fee.

Matt Bracken may be a fool, but Geoff wasn't. A gal like Fee was as rare and beautiful as this tiny paradise and well worth waiting for, if necessary.

"I appreciate your honesty, Fee. Obviously, I'm more than a little attracted to you, but if you're not ready to care about me that way, we'll stay friends for now."

He squeezed her shoulder to reassure her as Fee was biting her lip. "Don't worry, Fee. I'm fine. Let's enjoy the day. I've been here many times, but I've never explored the depths of the pool. Anything I missed?"

"Oh, a small family of water snakes, no muskrats, a few minnows, and frightened frogs."

Geoff watched her eyes light up as she launched into her favorite topic.

The lavender twilight faded to black as Fee hiked back to her cabin. Geoff had wanted to see her home, but she'd insisted that she'd often hiked this trail and knew it well. They had enjoyed the rest of the afternoon, even going swimming again. Geoff was the perfect gentleman, although she had caught a flash of raw desire in his eyes a few times.

As the forest fell silent for night, Fee's thoughts were noisy as she debated whether she should cancel Monday's field trip with Matt. She needed to complete the work, but what about her feelings for Matt? Could she conceal them?

—*—

Matt had spent Saturday preparing for the next week. He'd found a light air mattress and sleeping bag for Fee. His backpack would be lighter this time because a forestry helicopter pilot had agreed to drop off supplies at the blind during his patrol trip on Monday.

Matt tried to avoid thinking of Fee on her date with Geoff but failed miserably. Why was he unsettled by the thought of Fee moving on to another man?

His chance with Fee was blown when he had ended their relationship the day after they had been intimate. In any woman's book, that made him an asshole at least, but more damning, she had also risked her life searching for him that night.

What did he expect her to do? Forgive him and go on with the fling? She was more likely to forgive the wolf who attacked him.

She still had heat for him — no one kisses a man like Fee did him without an unmistakable yen for the guy. But hell, it could be a passing sexual urge that any man, but especially Geoff, could meet the need.

Geoff likely checked off all of Fee's 'perfect guy' boxes. He was a decent man, from all reports, who loved and protected nature and worse yet, a charming horny guy — and she was nearly naked in a bathing suit with him today. It was no great stretch to imagine what was going on at that picnic. Matt fought to get the images out of his mind of what had happened when he had Fee alone, wet in her bathing suit.

Matt looked up at the fading twilight. Should he check that Fee got home? Or should he mind his own business? She hadn't been off somewhere fighting wild animals, nothing more than on a date with Geoff Halloran. Matt swore and slammed out of the cabin.

Chapter 17

5:20 a.m. was a lousy time to be up when a person had little sleep. Fee was sitting on the lower step by her backpack and bags of equipment. Her eyes closed, her head resting on the railing, too tired to worry about anything — any man — anymore.

"It looks like you had a late night, Fee. Anyone I know?"

"Hmm, what? You're here already? What time is it?" Fee stood up, rubbing her eyes.

"5:30 a.m. It's time to leave if we want to get to the blind today — that's if you can stay awake?"

"Oh, sorry. I didn't sleep well last night. I'll be fine, just nightmares. Must have been my lousy cooking." Fee tried to look more alert as she shouldered her backpack while Matt stuffed the rest of her equipment in his pack.

In minutes, she was marching down the trail at a brisk pace.

Matt watched her perky tight butt bounce in front of him, her red ponytail swinging like a foxes' tail. A smile twitched at his lips, the surest way to motivate Fee was to accuse her of weakness. As usual, she had on her field outfit of camouflage pants and hat. Her waist was bristling with a bear spray can, knife sheath, flashlight, and small camera case. He looked closer, where was her pistol?

"Did you forget your weapon?"

"No, I have it in my pack. I need my camera handy as we hike because I want to take photos of the iridescent beetles along this trail. Anyway, you have your rifle in case of a nosey visitor with sharp teeth."

"Nice to hear you have faith in my ability to defend us."

"Don't be too pleased. Last time, if I remember, I rescued you."

"I'd be impressed if I had needed rescuing."

"You gave a rather convincing performance, what with all that limping and being chased by wolves. Who knew it was all fake? How did you talk the wolves into going along with your scheme?"

"I thought by now, you were aware of the power of my mighty charms?"

The banter continued, ending with them laughing and relaxing in each other's company.

By lunchtime, both were perspiring from the uphill hike. At a flat spot near a small, fast-flowing stream, they dropped their packs on the ground.

Fee peeled off her boots and socks and rolled up her pants to her knees. "That water looks inviting. I'm going to soak my feet." She plunked down on the riverbank by a tree, stuck her hot feet in the crystal water, and sighed in sheer relief. She wriggled her toes, and minnows swam up to investigate as she giggled with pleasure.

"Room for two?" Placing his rifle on the bank beside him, Matt sat beside her submerging his feet, his hip snug by Fee's, sending delicious ripples up her body. She fought the urge to lean on him. She turned sideways as he was passing her a sandwich, jerked to grab it, missed, her body tipping toward the water. Matt's arms went around her, pulling her back, the sandwich bag floating away.

For a few seconds, Fee allowed herself to inhale Matt's spicy male scent of pine and clean sweat while Matt buried his face in her silky hair, sniffing a natural scent that was all Fee. He could feel her chest rise and fall. He released her, gazed down at her upturned face, his eyes a magnet drawing her.

Fee jerked her head away.

"Well, there goes *your* sandwich. That'll teach you not to startle a gal. Can I have *my* sandwich now?" Her bantering tone was back. She jumped up and scampered over to her boots and socks. That was a close call. She'd better be a lot more careful, or Matt would figure out she still had the hots for him — more than the hots, damn it. Without a doubt, she sucked at getting over flings.

For the rest of the afternoon, Matt led the way, slowing the pace when he realized that Fee was falling behind, running more on determination than energy. She was also distracted, not her usual buoyant self, but he couldn't read her thoughts at all.

Fee, dead tired when the blind came in sight, sank down on the grass and gulped the last of her water. Nothing less than a starving wolf attack could make her move for the next thirty minutes. She stripped off her jacket and waist attachments and then stretched out under a tree.

Matt checked the supplies stacked under the blind platform. The helicopter pilot must have had help carrying them because the two wooden crates were heavy with months' worth of supplies. He turned to ask Fee if she was hungry, but she was fast asleep, her head and neck at an odd angle on her pack.

—*—

Fee woke from her deep sleep on a bed. A pale pink light leaked in from the window slats. She realized she was sleeping on a foamy on the storage chest with a fluffy blanket covering her. There was only one way she got here — Matt must've carried her. Where was he? She was fully clothed minus her boots. Well, that was a good sign. He was sticking to his commitment to behave as a colleague and nothing more.

"You're awake, good. I bet you're hungry too." Matt stepped through the doorway. "If you're ready to get up, I'll fire up the propane stove. We'll have wieners, beans, and biscuits. I left the rest of the food in the crates outside until tomorrow."

He looked fresh with his inky hair wet, curling around his ears. His tight white T-shirt highlighted his broad shoulders, his bronzed face and maple sugar eyes were full of energy. Did that man ever get tired? And why did he have to look totally edible?

"Dogs and beans sound yummy. Thanks for moving me. I must have passed out." Fee stood up for a stretch. Reaching up on her tiptoes, her T-shirt rode up, baring her belly button as she extended her arms.

Matt watched her, trying not to enjoy the charming view and failing. "Your neck was so crooked that I had to move you to a better bed. I called your name, but you didn't wake up." He could still feel the curve of her body as he carried her up the stairs. Her face was sweetly vulnerable as she slept.

Matt smiled at her as she rolled up the foamy and popped open the chest to get the stove. He appreciated that she was a "can-do" gal who pitched in with the chores.

"It looks like you've had a swim. I'd love one before we eat. Do you mind waiting?"

Matt felt his temperature rising as his body responded to the peek show that flashed in his mind of the lovemaking that followed their last swim. The look he gave Fee could melt steel.

Fee's cheeks bloomed bright rose as her mind treated her to the same images and sensations. Her heart was tap dancing, and her breath was keeping time.

Holy shit! She could jump Matt, and to hell with her emotions. Her heart was only one organ of many in her body, and the rest were ready to get back to the party.

Fee grabbed her bathing suit from her backpack, rushed out the door and down the stairs, sprinting for the water. She couldn't have run faster if she was trying to outrun an enraged badger. When she reached the river, she jumped in fully clothed. To hell with changing, she needed to chill —now!

Matt watched her from the deck. That was one way to chill down the libido, but how often could they jump in the river in a day? No question, mutual passion was still there. He was ready for her. But she refused to give in to her need.

A half an hour later, when Fee returned, Matt had supper ready. He stepped outside without comment to let her change into dry clothes. They ate in a strained silence, both ignoring the purple giraffe with pink spots in the room.

"Will you be observing tonight, Fee?"

"It's late. I'll only set up my night telescope. I'll work for an hour, I think. I want to be up before dawn to catch the early morning action by the river."

"In that case, I'll get your air mattress and sleeping bag out because I may be asleep when you finish. I'll do the dishes tonight."

It was about an hour later when Fee tiptoed into the room. Matt was fast asleep, his back turned away from her. Her bed was made up by the window, a pillow on the sleeping bag, and a blanket was folded nearby with her full water bottle next to it. She undressed by the light of a single candle left burning in a can on the window ledge. She blew it out and slipped into the shivery sleeping bag.

Before she fell asleep, she allowed herself one moment of yearning for the heat of Matt's muscled back to cuddle up to before she told her mind to 'shut up and go to sleep.'

Chapter 18

The next few days were busy, and the professional courtesy and tone were well in place. Fee had checked off her list several shy creatures who never ventured out of this part of the forest, while Matt had gone to the far-flung blinds to check on his data recorders, replacing the disks and repairing where needed.

Fee floated on her back, breathing in the sweet scent of wildflowers released by the blistering heat of the late summer sun. Matt would enjoy this, too, but if he returned now, she figured he would wait to swim until she was out of the water.

He had surprised her by his commitment to stick to their agreement, making no moves to rekindle their past intimacy. Even more unusual was he turned his back to her when she changed for bed at night and when she dressed in the morning.

Thunderclouds rolled in, dyeing the sky a bruised purple. Fee scrambled to the shore. The hut windows and door were open to allow the breeze to blow through. *Their equipment was exposed to the coming storm.*

She barely got the window slates closed before the first mighty crack of thunder. The wind rattled the shutters as a lightning bolt struck the deck, shaking the structure and igniting the deck boards that were as dry as tinder. The thunder roared overhead, but there was no rain. Fanned by the wind, the fire on deck was two feet high and spreading. No way could Fee fight it.

She raced back inside and began throwing her camera equipment and sketchbooks into her pack together with Matt's data disks. Anything in the metal storage locker trunk should be safe. She tore it open, grabbed the small tent, a sleeping bag, and the stove. She threw a frying pan and pot out the door, narrowly missing Matt's head as he rushed up the stairs.

"What the . . . are you all right?"

"Yes. Grab the stove and the water bag. I've got your disks."

They worked feverishly running up and down the stairs carrying equipment, the smoke burning their eyes. Within ten minutes, the hut filled with blinding smoke as flames engulfed the deck. They could do nothing now but stand back, surrounded by what they had salvaged, and watch the blind burn.

Matt's radio crackled. "This is Fire Emergency Service. We've spotted smoke in your area. Report."

"Lightning has hit Outlook Blind #14, and it's burning. It'll be gone before you can get a water bomber here unless it starts raining in the next few minutes."

"Roger, report in 10 minutes, sooner if it rains. We'll order the water bomber to deployment readiness."

Matt clipped the radio to his waist and turned to Fee. Black soot striped her yellow bathing suit and legs. With her big eyes watering from the smoke, she looked like a depressed bumblebee. A smile tugged at his lips, and he moved to put his arm around her but stopped himself.

"Let's get this gear under shelter before it rains." He filled his arms, stowing the gear under the tightly woven branches of an enormous nearby spruce. Fee followed, lugging as much as she could.

Rain pummeled them as they dove into a small space near the trunk of the spruce. Fee landed halfway onto Matt's lap, bumping her head into his chin. They peered over the gear at the steaming ruin of the blind as the rain fell like the blast from a fire hose.

"Matt, before you call Emergency services, please don't request an evacuation for me today. I want to stay."

"Are you sure? It'll be primitive accommodations from now on. You realize that we must share a small tent?"

"Yes, it will be close quarters, but we're doing fine as professionals. I'm not concerned. I haven't finished my work, and there may not be another opportunity." Fee beamed her highest wattage grin up at him, her teeth snow white in her sooty face.

"That's true. I won't return here until late fall. I may even finish my research before then. Okay, if you're sure, Fee, you can stay for the week. Let's get camp set up when we have a break in the rain."

Matt couldn't help smiling down at her dirty face. Too often, he wanted to pull her into his arms and kiss her or sit with his arm around her as she leaned into him. For days, he'd pretended they were almost strangers, getting out into the field early in the morning and staying away most of the day.

Well, that technique was useless now. How was he going to avoid blowing the whole arrangement while sharing such close quarters? The same sleeping bag?

When the small tent was up under the giant spruce tree, and the gear safe inside, there was room left for one foamy and sleeping bag.

"I guess I could try sleeping outside, Fee, but by the look of those clouds, the rain isn't finished yet." Matt's deep eyes locked onto her.

"No, we'll have to manage tonight even if we are squished. Let's figure out supper. I'm starving." Focusing on the practical situation was the best policy. No use her worrying about the necessity of sleeping almost on top of one another.

"I threw food in one of these bags." Fee hunted through the pile to see what they could find to eat and came up with freeze-dried chili pouches, a bruised banana, plus a small packet of strawberry powder to add to water. No coffee or tea.

"We have one small tank of propane, and we need it for our lantern. As of tomorrow, we better cook over a campfire and not use the stove," Matt advised.

"Hey, no problem. I'm a whiz at charred campfire fish."

"You haven't roughed it until you've dined on my rubbery, rabbit stew."

"Should we see if we can salvage any food supplies from the crates tomorrow?"

"Absolutely!"

A boom of thunder drowned their laughter. The storm wasn't finished with them yet.

Fee shivered in her bathing suit. "I'd sure like to have a hot shower about now, but I'd settle for a small pot of heated water to wash off the soot." The rain began to patter on the ground, building up speed until it was pouring again.

"Looks like it's Mother Nature's shower for us. Hard to say what clothes I have left to wear. I better keep these dry for now."

They both crawled out of the tent and stood up under the sheltering tree.

Matt unbuttoned his shirt, flipped off his t-shirt, unzipped his jeans, and dropped them. As he put his thumbs on the waistband of his jockey shorts, he raised his eyebrow at Fee, who stood watching. Turning his back, he yanked down his shorts and walked out into the warm, steady rain. His muscled body gleamed with water as he raised his arms.

Fee stepped out from under the tree. She needed a shower, and it was being provided. Matt wasn't shy, why should she be?

The rain pelted down as she peeled off her bathing suit then began to move, twirling in the deluge. Her nipples peaked with the air rushing around them, her hair hung in auburn skeins to her rounded bottom-cheeks. The rain massaged her body with a thousand tiny fingertips as the soot washed away. She inhaled the wet earth scent as the silky grass stroked her dancing feet.

The rain dissolved her cares, and, for this moment, fire and high water didn't matter. Her delight in her connection with nature was all that existed.

Matt stood mesmerized by Fee's dance. He had peeked quickly to check on her, but now he couldn't stop watching. She was freedom, passion, and love. Like the water sirens called out to seafarers, her spirit called out to him.

Fee slowed and then stood with her eyes closed, her chest heaving.

"Unless you're a 'professional' water sprite, I believe that your naked dance can be classified as 'unprofessional.' Therefore, I can do this." Matt swept Fee's slippery body against his wet, muscular torso, his arousal urgent. He claimed her, thrusting his tongue through her parted lips, tasting her freshness.

Fee sighed and slipped her tongue into his hot mouth, eager to answer his invitation.

Matt groaned and lifted her off the ground, his hands cupping her bottom, her legs encircled his waist, as her sex opened to him.

"God, I want you, Fee. Can I?

"Huh . . . yes!"

Matt lowered her slightly, then pushed hard into her wet and willing cleft, her satin folds swathing his shaft. Fee purred as they synced their rhythm. It was as if her rain dance had continued on, but now she had snared her sailor. Their climax was applauded by a flash of light and rumbling thunder.

As Fee slid off Matt, he grabbed her shoulders and tipped her face up to his, peered into her eyes. "Plainly, Mother Nature approves, Fee. Please don't have regrets. Blame it on this wild day. We needed to let off steam. We can go back to 'professional' status, I promise."

She leaned into his sheltering body and hugged him. The glow of their lovemaking still radiated through her body, creating waves of pleasure. There was no way she wanted to dispel that loving feeling with a difficult discussion. Every part of her wanted him, but she knew she shouldn't rekindle their fling. But for now, she didn't want to think.

Fee stepped back from him shaking her head. "Let's deal with what we need right now. If my clothes are burned, I might have left to wear only my wet bathing suit and rubber water shoes." She shivered.

Matt passed his damp shirt and slipped on his jeans. "You're right. We can talk later. The rain has stopped, and it's getting dark. We need to get ready for a night outside of the blind and its protection."

He lit the lantern, and they sorted through the heap of stuff inside the tent. Fee found her cargo pants and a pair of underwear, her hiking boots, but no bra. Matt was luckier because he'd been fully dressed when the fire started, although he didn't have much else other than what he was wearing. They searched together in awkward silence.

"Well, we have a limited wardrobe, but at any rate, we're clean." Matt laughed ruefully and then even harder when he peered at Fee.

In bare legs, wearing just Matt's oversized cargo shirt, Fee looked like a shipwrecked survivor who had escaped the god Neptune's wrath. Her hair, already drying into a mass of tangled curls, stood out from her head about six inches in the lightening charged air. Fee joined the laughter when she saw Matt dangle in the air a single sock, and a dirty T-shirt.

The tension relieved, they decided to call this day done, get some sleep, and deal with anything else in the morning. The foamy and sleeping bag didn't have room to lie flat, the sides rode up on the piles of their gear.

"I can turn on my side, Fee, and then you can lie flat."

"Oh, for heaven's sake, let's both sleep on our sides. We've already been a hell of a lot more non-professional than that today." Fee, wrapped in his cargo shirt, turned on her side. Matt, wearing his jockeys, curled his frame around her. Fee gave up thinking and relaxed into his body heat and the comfort of his arms. In no time, she was fast asleep, as was Matt, who was breathing into her hair.

Chapter 19

Matt jerked awake to the sound of a sharp pinging on metal that sounded like sniper fire. The sun streamed in through the mesh window. Fee was snuggled into his chest, her hand resting on his heart, mouth puckered, blowing softly on him. He hated to move, but he'd better investigate what was going on outside the tent. A crash and a harsh cry made him leap up and pull on his jeans. He grabbed the rifle, opened the canvas flap, and fired.

"Sorry, Fee, but we have company. The scavengers are already at our food." He stepped outside while Fee blinked and then fumbled around for clothing.

Soon she too was outside, watching Matt chase off a flock of bold ravens. They'd been at work for a while, as evidenced by the mess of pasta noodles spread around, and the torn soup pouches oozing their contents. The ravens were too curious to eat one thing at a time.

"I guess it's the early bird that gets the soup and noodles. It can't be later than 6 a.m., but I'm as hungry as they are."

Matt's shirt hung to her knees, bright yellow rubber shoes adorning her feet. On one side of her head, her hair was a tangled nest ready for a family of robins, but her hair lay flat on the other side. As she stretched, the sleeves in the oversized shirt flapped like wings as the hem rose, revealing her tanned thighs.

Matt looked at her and chuckled. A man had to admire a woman who woke up in good humor despite bad luck and didn't care if she looked like a miniature clown. Fee was damn adorable at her worst.

He wished he could stroke and kiss her until she was breathless to satisfy a different appetite, but she hadn't canceled the 'professional conduct' agreement. No choice. He had to assume it was back in effect.

"Fee, let's have breakfast then get to work to prevent our feathered friends from treating our supplies as the local grocery store. Anyway, they found instant coffee for us."

They boiled the water, sweetening the coffee with honey dripping out of a pouch abandoned by the birds, pried open a can of corn beef, and shared the crackers left in a pecked open box.

"Okay, let's see what the damage is, I'll test the steps." Matt put his weight on the bottom step and climbed. Fee followed behind.

The rain had come fast enough to save most of the structure. The observation deck had a great gaping hole, as did the hut wall closest to the fire. The best news was that the metal roof and supports were fine, as was the floor, and the equipment inside the storage box was undamaged.

"I don't normally volunteer to do a man's laundry, but I'll make you a deal. You get the wall repaired, and I'll wash your clothes with mine."

"I accept your deal and raise the stakes. You catch us trout for lunch, and I'll try to fix deck this afternoon."

The whole place reeked of smoke, including Fee's clothes in her duffle bag that hung on a peg by the door. Fee changed into smoky shorts and her own T-shirt and found a bar of soap in the trunk. It was a laundry day.

Outside, the August sun bore down on Matt as he chopped logs for boards. Perspiration gleamed like oil on his chest, arms, and legs even though he was stripped to his black jockey shorts and hiking boots. He was a creditable replicate of a rugged male underwear model, an alluring sight.

Fee yearned to stay and admire the view, but she knew where that led. Shouldering her bag and carrying an armful of clothing, she trudged down to the stream and

sloshed right into the water. For once, being fully clothed in water made sense.

Two hours later, Matt's clothes were fluttering in the tree with hers, including her bras and underwear. Her bathing suit, washed, was back on; she'd wear it until her clothes dried. She pulled her clean hair into a wet ponytail, errant curls escaping around her face.

An attempt to catch a fish for lunch had failed. Scared off, they hid under the banks not likely to bite now until late in the day. She'd have to figure out another way to keep her side of the bargain.

Matt sat on the top step swigging water, back in his cargo pants and T-shirt. He'd be happy if Fee's clothes took forever to dry, he loved that bathing suit on her.

"I take it that's a victory drink. You patched the wall?"

"You doubt? Come admire the results." He bowed Fee into the hut to examine the hole that had disappeared under wooden boards.

Fee inspected the wall, "Not bad for an amateur. "

"Amateur? I swung a hammer on local construction projects for most of my summer breaks at school. And speaking of amateurs, where's the fish?" He placed his hands on his hips, and mock glared at her.

"Funny, you should ask. Not only did the trout refuse to co-operate with weak excuses about the heat, but they also whined about all my thrashing about in the water and, worse yet, about the soap bubbles. They sneered when I said that the soap was biodegradable."

"In other words, they didn't bite."

"I like to think it was because of their lazy attitude and not an aspersion against my formidable fishing skills."

"Their attitude doesn't get you off the hook. You must pay a forfeit penalty." He waggled his eyebrows like an old-fashioned villain.

"Please be merciful, kind sir." Fee gasped and put her palm on her forehead.

"You will help me this afternoon and be in charge of procuring food and cooking our meals today and tomorrow. Plus, one of those meals must be fresh fish."

"You are too cruel, sir. Is there no other way?" She winked at him saucily.

"I will reduce the penalty for a kiss from your fair lips."

Fee sashayed over to him, jumped up, and kissed his nose. He grabbed her and drew her into his arms, his mouth capturing hers in a hot, wild kiss.

Fee pushed him away, "Back off, buddy. Go jump in the river!"

"Damn, Fee, we were joking, well, flirting. I'm sorry, I know we're supposed to be back on a 'work only' basis, but . . ." He stopped because Fee was laughing.

"I pushed you away because you stink of smoke, Matt, and yes, we shouldn't be kissing. We'll talk about that later, but right now, go wash and take the soap with you. You'll find clean clothes hanging on the tree. I'll make lunch."

Matt sniffed his T-shirt and made a face. "You have a point. I'd hate for you to reject me because I reek like Smokey the Bear. I'll take the water bag with me."

—*—

The small campfire heated the grill, a pot of canned stew bubbled away, and the biscuit mix was ready to go in the frying pan.

"I should write you up for an illegal campfire."

Fee set a pan on the grill then stood up. Geoff enveloped her in a bear hug, "Thank God, you're safe! I heard about the fire this morning. Did you get burned?" He drew back and peered into her face, his hands on her waist.

Fee could see the real fear in his eyes, and smiled up at him, "Not even a bit crisp, thanks to luck and the rain." She leaned in and hugged him. "I'm fine, no worries."

"Sorry to disturb you. Nice to see you again, Geoff." Back from the river, Matt looked anything but pleased to see Geoff Halloran with his arms around Fee.

"Join us for lunch? I'll open another can of stew." Fee pulled away from Geoff, squeezing his arm.

"Sure, I'd like that. I've worked up an appetite hiking in here, but let me contribute to the meal. I packed in food; in case you were short after the fire."

He smiled at Fee, his blue eyes sending a private message. "I also brought those strawberries you love." He knelt down by his large backpack, pulled out a cooler bag, extracted strawberries, a small container of cream, and a package of hotdogs.

"Now, we're talking gourmet! Thanks, Geoff, you're a lifesaver. We'll roast these hotdogs and have a real fire survival feast."

They laughed together as Matt observed them. They had an affectionate connection, were at ease with each other. Fee was plainly enjoying flirting with Geoff. What was their relationship anyway?

A man didn't hike for hours through rough terrain to bring strawberries to a woman unless he had a compelling reason. No prizes for figuring out what *that* reason was.

Geoff offered to help with repairing the hole in the deck, and Matt couldn't refuse. He and Geoff were able to make short work of a job that would have taken Fee and him all afternoon. Geoff even volunteered to help Matt carry the equipment back into the hut, sparing Fee even more work.

Finally, Matt insisted Geoff leave in time to make it back to his base before nightfall. No invitation was issued for Geoff to spend the night at the blind. Geoff went, but not before he hugged Fee, whispered something in her ear that made her giggle and kiss his cheek.

Fee had to admit to herself that she'd relished the afternoon entertainment watching the two men work. Both men had stripped off their shirts, and their rippling muscles and buffed physiques were a pleasure to behold. They may not have been on her list of creatures to sketch, but she was happy to add them.

She'd sat under the tree sketching, too far away to hear their conversation, but she could tell it was intense. At one point, they had stood up and backed away from each other like they were squaring off for a fight, and then they stopped talking altogether. She'd captured Geoff's challenging expression and Matt's fierce one. Were they discussing her?

Chapter 20

It had been a quiet night.

Conversation over supper was sparse, which Fee assumed was Matt's fatigue from working hard all day in the heat. When she came in from her observations on deck, her bed was made up on the floor, and Matt was sleeping with his back to her. The "professional" rules were back in place without discussion.

Well, that was nice! After mind-blowing sex on one night with a gal, boot her back to her own bed the next. Talk about being volcanic one day and glacial the next.

Fee lay in her sleeping bag, trying to control her temper. What was it with him? Maybe, she didn't want the whole "hands-off" thing anymore, but Matt never bothered even asking if she'd changed her mind. To hell with him, he'd rejected her for the last time.

She turned on her side and demanded that her emotions and her body let her sleep, but since when did they listen to her?

—*—

When the morning light peeped through the slats, Fee was already on the deck, waiting for the dawn, her eyes heavy-lidded from lack of sleep.

Matt stepped out into the fresh air. He checked to see if Fee was fishing, but she was sitting on the bench, arms around her knees, staring out into space.

"I'll try my hand at fishing today if you like."

"No, thank-you. I keep my commitments." Fee brushed by him, picked up her fishing rod, and stomped down the steps, her small back rigid.

Matt watched her cross the meadow to the river. The wolf packs had retreated deeper in the zone, but he was still relieved to see bear spray clipped to her waistband.

The thought struck him, *that never before had he felt this protective of a woman.* But then, Fee was a woman willing to take on wolves, bears, and fire, ready to take risks daily. She was a fiery blend of courage, humor, and passion wrapped in an enticing body with a pretty face. No wonder Geoff was smitten with her.

His confrontation with Geoff yesterday remained fresh in his mind.

Geoff had stopped hammering, his eyes cold, his mouth in a grim line. "Fee can't hear us, so I want to talk straight with you about Fee. I realize she has feelings for you, but she's not your type of woman."

He stood up, and Matt followed suit.

"I don't recall asking you for advice on my personal life, Geoff, and I sure as hell don't regard you as an expert on what woman is the right one for me." Matt glared and widened his feet into a fighter's stance, still keeping his hands at his sides.

Matt's open hostility shocked Geoff. For God's sake, he didn't want to fight him. Geoff measured Matt's swinging distance and stepped back. "Look, I don't like to get involved in this crap, but you must recognize that Fee's a quality gal who doesn't play games."

"Yes, I do, but how's Fee's personal business now your business too? What are you getting at?" Matt's voice was rising. He glanced over at Fee, who watched them. He dropped his voice to a low growl. "Geoff, I suggest you drop the topic, and back the hell off — now."

"Listen, I'm not judging you, but she's one of us, trying hard in her own way to protect nature. I'm sure you respect her, at least professionally. Do you honestly want to hurt her?"

"Are you sure that you're altruistic, Geoff? Is protecting Fee your motive, or are you trying to eliminate the competition? What have you been saying to her about me?" Matt's voice took on a threatening tone.

"You don't come up in our conversations, but I admit I admire Fee, and I've told her that. Be honest, man. You're a guy who doesn't like commitment. You will crush her and leave her." Geoff paused, not sure if he would have to duck a punch.

Matt crossed his arms — he'd better chill his temper. He took two deep breaths then spoke. "Geoff, you may think Fee needs your interference in her love life, but she doesn't. I respect her ability to make up her own mind, and you should too."

"Oh, I respect Fee's judgment, but she's vulnerable because of her feelings for you. If you could actually love her, I'd wish you both the best of luck and bow out. But let's not pretend you'll ever commit to Fee. We both know that won't happen, Matt."

The gauntlet cast down, they stopped talking.

Matt was brought back to the present with Fee arriving back with her catch. Soon they were eating fried trout, buttered bread, and honey for breakfast. They drank their black coffee, no one speaking.

Fee broke the silence. "Matt, could we go to the blind nearer the mountain? Geoff said that there are at two least cougar dens with cubs in that area."

"Geoff is a fount of knowledge on this part of the Zone, I see."

"Is he wrong? The firefighters reported them." Fee ignored his sarcastic tone.

"No, he's right this time, but I thought you already sketched the mother and cubs. Or did you devote your time to Geoff last Saturday?"

What? Now he's jealous? Even though last night, he'd barely acknowledged her presence?

Fee stayed focused. "I did, but I want to catch the cougars in action."

"That's dangerous and likely at night."

"But is it possible?"

"Yes. The blind's in a tree that's netted to keep the cougars out. We'd have to spend the night in the blind, and you won't like the savageness you may witness."

"If you mean a kill, I have observed that with other predators before now. It's part of nature, the circle of life. I can handle it."

"I'd be in charge, and you'd have to accept my decisions without question. It's too dangerous otherwise. I need your word on that."

Fee's face lit up with a grateful smile. "I'm not the expert there, you are. I will respect your decisions, I promise."

"All right, I'm taking that as a commitment. I need to go there anyway before we return home. We'll leave

today. This dry weather might not last, plus there's a full moon tonight. It's about 6 miles from here."

It was hard not to respond to Fee's smile. Matt's heart felt like it was being punched. After wrestling with his conscience last night, he'd decided that the way to be fair to Fee was to let her go.

He hated to agree with Geoff, but committing to a relationship felt like ripping open a healed wound. He never wanted to experience once more the world of pain that he and his father had endured when his mother deserted them. If he couldn't commit to a relationship with Fee, then he needed to keep his distance.

"This blind is much smaller than number 14, and we won't cook — no smelly food at all. Keep in mind we must stay quiet all night. Cougars hunt at night and in the early morning. We need to get to the blind by early afternoon."

He must be crazy agreeing to this, but he couldn't refuse to help Fee. He owed her the opportunity to observe the cougars after all her efforts. But now that he'd decided that he didn't want to hurt her further by continuing their intimate relationship, it was even harder to be around her. At the tree blind, they would spend the night in a tiny space together.

An hour later, they'd packed, secured the blind from scavengers, and were hiking down a trail with Matt leading. Fee was surprised he had agreed to take her with him. Since Geoff left, Matt was a different guy, almost surly. He'd lost all interest in a conversation, avoiding her as much as possible.

She wanted to believe that Matt cared for her because he had such tenderness in his lovemaking and was fierce in his protection of her. It couldn't be purely a fling for him, could it? Yet, he did seem to find it easy to retreat to a colleague relationship.

One thing for sure was that she'd left fling territory a while ago. Yep, she'd fallen for another man who would abandon her. How would she endure being in a confined space with him tonight? They'd be bumping into each other all the time.

As they hiked, Fee allowed the beauty freely given to ease her heart. The wildflowers were a riot of blues, yellows, oranges, and reds. Wild pink roses perfumed the baking summer air as fat bumblebees hummed, drunk with nectar.

In the shady spots, the ferns waved like the sea, nature's last hooray before autumn's chill led to winter's hush of snow.

Matt turned to suggest they stop at a shady spot but didn't speak. Fee's face was radiant. Her eyes glowed, and the corners of her mouth tipped up in a smile. She was at peace here deep in the wilderness.

"Are we stopping, Matt? I could devour a snack and a drink."

"Yes, let's take a break."

Fee handed him a fish sandwich made from trout seasoned with mustard. "I thought we should finish this morning's trout. It won't be any good when we get back." She sat on a log, chomped her sandwich, and drank water that she'd flavored with orange crystals.

Matt sputtered when he drank from his water bottle.

"I guess I should have mentioned that I've upgraded our water." There was no mistaking the mischief in her face.

"Lucky, I like orange flavor. Are there any other surprises to expect?"

"It's not a surprise if you expect it."

"I regret assigning you the food packing."

They reached the blind an hour later. It was in a tall aspen tree close to a mountain stream, a great spot for animal watching. The tree was denuded of branches up to the blind. They rope-climbed the twenty feet, Matt going up first and then pulling up his heavy pack attached to the rope, followed by Fee's lighter bag. Fee nimbly climbed up using the line.

"It's been a while since I've done that." She flopped down on the small deck panting.

"You've earned your monkey badge for climbing a tree without branches." He grinned at her proud face.

"A gal can't have enough of those, but this seems high for an observation post."

"Cougars have been known to jump vertically in a single leap up to 18 feet."

Fee was quiet for a moment, "How far can they leap across from another tree?"

"Approximately twenty feet — that's why we netted the blind and cut the branches away from it. That doesn't mean they can't still reach us. Their legs are like giant steel springs."

Fee glance over to her pack, where her pistol was kept. Maybe she should be wearing it. She frowned.

"They won't be interested in us unless we draw attention to ourselves or appear to be a threat. We won't do either."

"Oh, I'm not worried. Nothing wrong with being prepared, though."

Matt busied himself sorting their stuff, his face turned away from Fee to hide his concern. No one but an idiot would feel safe in this environment. Already he regretted bringing her here. The last thing he wanted was to put her in peril — again. He radioed their location to Forestry Services, the standard protocol.

They peered out of the blind's narrow slats cut into the wooden walls on three sides. The fourth side was a solid wall. Most of the critters were sleeping in the afternoon sun's heat, and Fee was nodding too.

"Why don't you take a nap? Nothing will happen for hours yet."

Matt dropped to the floor, stretched out his legs, and supported his back with the wall. Fee joined him, slumped alongside his shoulder as sleep overtook her. He reached out, pulled her into a more comfortable position with his arm around her. For a while, he watched her face, her silky lashes fanned out on her cheeks, her lips slightly parted, and her hair sticking up to tickle his nose. He yearned to kiss her, to draw all that sweetness into him, but he simply patted her hair down with his fingertips. She stirred in her sleep and snuggled in closer.

Fee came awake to Matt shaking her shoulder. The room was in deep shadow. Where was she? "What's going on?" Her voice was loud.

"Shush, shush… there's movement below us." Matt whispered.

She inched to the window slats. She could hear scrabbling as if a wild thing was climbing up the tree, *their tree*. "What is it? Can you see it?" She tried to see past Matt. He moved to let her stand in front of him.

"Smaller animals are hiding. They're afraid. A few squirrels, and it looks like a possum is scrambling up our tree. There must be a predator close by."

Fee spotted a small, brown furry face with shiny black button eyes as it peered at them. When she chuckled, the animal bolted, scampering up the netting, over the roof, and escaping farther up the tree.

"Well, that's one squirrel that won't be dinner tonight." Fee slid her night, goggles out of her backpack. As the twilight was fading fast, there should be action soon.

"I'm sure I'd see better outside on the platform than in the blind."

"The blind protects you. Also, the ledge is narrow, less than four feet wide."

"There's a guard rail. I'll sit on the edge of the platform and tie myself to the support strut."

"And dangle your legs over the ledge? And if a cougar sinks his teeth into your leg?"

"All right, if you put like that, I won't dangle. Can I lie down?"

"Yes, but first . . ."

Before Matt could utter another word, Fee darted out the door, stretched out on the deck on her tummy, legs bent at the knee toward her butt, clutching her night binoculars as she peered below the blind.

Matt followed her, his face tight with frustration, "Fee, you're too impulsive. You didn't do any safety checks before you came out of the blind. This is *not* a safe place. If a cougar were on the blind roof, he might have attacked you despite the net. Falling down on the deck like that makes you easy prey."

"Oh, but wouldn't we have heard him on the roof?"

"Possibly, but he could have been lying in wait for hours. We can't make assumptions out here."

"I am sorry, Matt. I got excited. What do you suggest we do now?" She stood up and touched his arm in apology, her tone contrite.

Matt released his breath, trying to relax. He fervently wished he hadn't brought her here. How was he going to keep Fee safe when her enthusiasm might get her killed?

"No cougar is up here right now. I'll stand watch with my rifle while you observe. But I don't want to shoot a cougar to protect you. Be alert, ready to move fast into the blind. Remember, we're not hidden from the big cats. They *know* we're here. They smelled us hours ago, but we're not the prey they're hunting. Let's keep it that way."

Chapter 21

2:30 a.m. This whole trip might be a failure. Fee had been lying out on the deck for hours, and nothing much had happened. The action tonight was a swooping owl capturing a small bat in his talons, and a fox chasing a rabbit in vain. Another elk wandered up to the stream to drink, a calf trailing behind her. Fee reckoned the whole herd would march by before the night was out. She stood up, put down her binoculars, and stretched.

Matt stretched too with his rifle slung over his shoulder, knocking his shoulder blades. "Nights can be quiet like this, but don't be discouraged. Cougars also like to hunt in the early morning."

They'd snacked on nuts and cheese earlier, but Fee's stomach growled, anyway.

"Hey, don't be scaring the wildlife," Matt whispered, smiling. "I'll see if I can find you a protein bar to chew.

He turned to go inside but froze when a shriek of pain split the air. He swung back to Fee.

Fee flung herself back down and focused on the scene below her.

A small elk calf, mewling in fear, was being dragged by the scruff of his neck up a nearby tree by a large male cougar. Immediately the cougar bit through its neck, and the calf went limp. The mother elk bugled below the tree, unable to help her baby. She circled the tree, her plaintive calls to her calf alerting the nearby bull elk of danger who barked a warning.

An elk herd grazing about twenty yards away panicked, rushing into the forest, cracking off branches. The mother huffed, then turned away to run after the crowd, but they were already far ahead.

With the calf wedged in the tree, the cougar leaped down, rushing after the elk, outpacing her. He sprang on her back, and sank his razor-sharp claws into her flanks, plunging his dagger-like canine teeth into her neck, severing her vertebrae and spinal column. The elk's legs buckled, and shortly the lone sound was the cougar's low growls as he feasted on her stomach.

Fee was glad she had eaten little. They were back inside the blind, and Matt had spread the sleeping bag out over a thin foamy mattress. Too unsettled to go to bed, she stood to stare out a window slat. She could hear wolf growls now — no doubt they were fighting the cougar for his kill.

Matt handed her a cup of tea from a thermos. Fee took a mouthful and sputtered. The drink was laced with whiskey.

"I had a feeling we might need a stronger drink than tea on this trip. Come and sit down beside me. It's late. You need to sleep." He patted the double sleeping bag.

Fee came over, passed him her cup, pulled off her boots, and fully clothed slid her legs into the sleeping bag. Sitting up, she tossed the whiskey tea back in one swallow.

"That poor mother stayed too long trying to protect her calf. It's what happened to my mother."

"What do you mean? Didn't both your parents die from an Ebola outbreak in the Congo?" He looked down at Fee's face. The moonlight revealed the unshed tears in her eyes. He reached out and put his arm around her, his heat seeping into her chilled shoulders.

"Yes, but they stayed too long because of me. I loved it there. I remember Mom and Dad telling me I had to leave, and my begging to stay."

"Oh, Fee, they wouldn't have stayed once they knew of the outbreak, no matter how much you begged. As scientists, they knew the danger. I suspect they were infected already. I'm sure your parents tried to protect you."

"That makes sense to an adult, but at eight years old, when they sent me home, and I never saw them again, it was like they deserted me. It's not logical, but I still expect to be left behind in relationships."

She turned her face away from him and sighed, "I'm going to sleep. Thanks for listening. Anymore whiskey and all my secrets would be revealed."

She slid down and curled onto her side, bumping his hip with her butt. How could *he* comfort her? Wasn't he planning on abandoning her too? Matt curled up next to her, his arms keeping her close to him, for tonight anyway.

—*—

Early morning, Matt struggled to extract himself from the sleeping bag without waking Fee. As usual, in her sleep, she had snuggled into him, trusting him. He hated to move and break the intimacy.

He crept out to the platform, returning quickly. Fee opened her eyes.

"It's early, Fee, about 6:00 a.m. We can't go yet. Wolves are eating the elk's carcass, plus the cougar is back up the tree. We may have to wait for hours, even another day."

Fee peered at Matt. He looked exhausted as if he hadn't slept at all.

It was crazy, but she felt refreshed, lighter in spirit than she had in a long time. Her confession to Matt of her dread of abandonment seemed to have broken the chain of fear around her heart. In a daring move, she had revealed her hidden demons to a man she loves, and that seemed to have banished them.

Playing it safe in relationships before now hadn't protected her from heartache. Most of the time, she was miserable, second-guessing the man's motives and intentions, always expecting pain. Fee resolved to live fully her present moments from now on.

No matter what happened, it had to be more fun than always being afraid of losing.

Breakfast was a shared pouch of cold baked beans, crackers, and the last of the cheese that Fee dug out of the food bag. They split a chocolate protein bar as they sat on the sleeping bag picnic style.

"It's not much, but we need to make our food stretch as far as we can because we can't fish or hunt here, nor have a fire." She licked the chocolate off her bottom lip.

"No problem, it's delicious to me. I was hungry."

Matt's swarthy morning beard bristles gave him the rakish look of a pirate. His black hair was tousled, curling around his ears, his shirt unbuttoned to the waist, and his bronzed chest chiseled beauty. His brawny, corded arms and large hands could easily weld a cutlass sword.

"Matt, if this is gourmet food, you'll be overcome with joy at eating cold spaghetti for lunch today. These field food pouches are no end of delight, Captain Black Jack."

Fee gave him a saucy look, reached over and scratched his beard, and then licked his neck, and nibbled his ear.

Matt gripped her shoulders and held her eyes as his tawny ones darkened with need. "Fee, I am aching for you, but making love will make things worse for you later."

"Matt, I'm done with my fears of rejection. Today, I'm alive and with a pirate as hot as cannon fire, surrounded by beasts that could tear us apart. What better time than now to enjoy the moment?"

She stood up, stripped off her shirt and jeans, unbuttoned her bra freeing her breasts, and then peeled off her panties. She flung back her unruly auburn hair, afire with the sunlight spilling in, her gray eyes bright and brimming with a challenge.

Matt growled and grabbed her by the waist. Kneeling, he pulled her close, then like a sculptor traced her body with his fingertips from her trim ankles to her neck, including all the parts never exposed in statues found in galleries. He tickled her navel with his tongue while his fingers stroked her mound, causing Fee to hum with pleasure, and then spread her legs wider.

Fee ran her fingers through Matt's dark hair, then gripped his shoulders hard as he parted her labia like a butterfly, licked it, and blew his soft breath on it, playing with its innermost bud with the tip of his tongue.

"Matt, take off your clothes now!"

Matt stood up, yanked his shirt off, flinging it down. Fee dropped to her knees, pulled his zipper down, pushing his jeans and jockeys down to the floor. In one swift movement, he kicked them away. Now, he stood naked before her, erect with arousal.

Fee took his hand and pulled him down to the bed onto his back, but as he reached for her, she stopped him.

"My turn." Time to pay homage to the sheer male beauty spread out before her. She stroked each contour of muscle and sinew, savored each with her tongue, then sucked and nipped his nipples. Fanning her hands on his flat stomach, her fingers drifted down to his soft curls twirling them around her fingers, teasing his manhood as she licked the tip and blew on it.

Matt groaned. "Fee, I want you now!"

She moved over him, opening her legs, leisurely engulfing his shaft with her body, her soft folds sliding down him like wet silk. Matt's fierce growl matched the wolves outside the blind.

Fee moved with the rhythm of life, ebbing and flowing, throwing her head back, lost in the utter joy of mating with the man she loved. She claimed this moment, no matter what tomorrow would bring.

The morning passed in a frenzy of lovemaking, exploring and daring to meet all desires, wishes, and needs. The more they made love, the more their passion increased. Finally, they both fell back, spent. Fee's head rested on Matt's shoulder while his hand rested on her bare stomach.

"I'm starving. Even that cold spaghetti would be good if I had the energy to rip the pouch open." Fee sighed.

"You haven't left me much energy, but I can manage that." Matt laughed, rose, and slid his jeans over his bare butt.

Fee pulled on his shirt and sat up as Matt brought the food over to the bed. They ate the spaghetti, and every morsel of food left, even drinking the last of the water.

"I better check on the situation outside. If we're going to make it back to the Outlook blind today, we should move pronto."

Matt slowly opened the door, the rifle ready. All was quiet, although if an entire pack of cougars had been sitting in wait on the deck, he wouldn't have noticed them until now. A close survey revealed that all the large predators were gone, probably sleeping in their dens. The tree by the stream was empty of the cougar and elk calf, and the bones of the mother elk were being picked clean by the crows.

When he came back in the blind, Fee was dressed and stuffing their packs. "Anything still out there?"

"Nope, we must have scared them all away this morning with our noise." He leered at Fee as she laughed.

"I'd love a good soak in the stream, but I'd prefer to wash in the river by the Outlook blind. This one has too much action even for me." Fee grimaced, the image of the mother and baby elk being slaughtered still fresh in her mind.

"I agree, a stream centered in a cougar and wolf hunting ground is not ideal for bathing. Let's head out while the big guys are resting in the midday heat."

Matt collected his data disks from the recorders in the tree, and they left. They made good time with the lighter packs, stopping once to rest by a narrow stream and fill their water bottles. They made it back to the blind by late afternoon and radioed their return to Search and Rescue.

The river washed away the dirt and dust, each of them soaping the other's back and more tender parts, and "tender" was a good description of those parts. Fee asked for a softer touch from Matt as the morning's activities had made her sensitive.

At sunset, they were sitting around the fire, finishing hot stew, buttered pan biscuits, and canned cherries.

Matt sighed, "A field trip to this blind will never be the same without you, Fee. Such creature comforts will be missed."

"The bar is low if my pan biscuits draw high praise. I'm not famous for my cooking skills."

"Today, everything tastes better." He waggled his eyebrows at Fee.

Matt was enjoying the ease between them and didn't want to say anything to change it, but she needed to hear how much he appreciated her. "I hope you realize I am admiring more than your biscuits?"

"The admiration is mutual, Matt, but I'd like an early night. I want to make a prompt start on my sketching tomorrow while everything is fresh in my mind. Now, I need to catch up on sleep. I barely got three hours last night."

Matt was more than a little surprised that Fee didn't want to pursue the topic. That she hadn't taken the opening to question his feelings about her. Although her fearless 'seize the moment' attitude toward him was exhilarating to be around — and he figured he'd be a fool to question it — it still made him uneasy. How far would she go with this new attitude?

Fee stretched and began to gather up the pots and dishes for washing in the morning, the deal being whoever fished, washed last night's dishes while the other one got the fire going, and made the coffee.

The sleeping bag, cushioned by the air mattress on top of the storage chest, was a feather bed compared to the thin foamy and hard floor of the other blind. Tonight, there was no discussion of sleeping arrangements. They both climbed in, cuddled up, and fell asleep.

Chapter 22

Fee wasn't sure that this morning's grisly sketches of the cougar attack would be accepted for a school science textbook, but she believed they should be. Nature's cycle of life and death was natural, not wrong. Her new wisdom whispered that relationships, too, had a lifespan, some shorter than others.

Matt, back from his final checks and data collection for this field trip, stood off observing Fee as she worked in the shade under the spreading branches of the spruce tree. She set down her charcoal as her gaze shifted to at least a mile in the distance.

"How's the sketching going?" He walked over and glanced at her drawing. Her sketch was an exact depiction of the events, adding no judgment. In the corner of one illustration, she had sketched a mother cougar with her two cubs. "I see that you want to present the two perspectives, the mother elk and calf juxtaposed with the mother cougar and cubs. The cougar attack doesn't seem wrong, purely for survival."

Fee touched his hand and beamed her thousand-watt smile up at him in appreciation. "I'm glad that's the idea you got from the positioning of the sketches. It's what I want to portray."

Matt put his hands on each side of her face and kissed her lips. He loved her empathy with nature's cycles and realities — and her smile that he couldn't resist. Her eyes seemed wet, but likely that was a trick of the light.

"Fee, do you need to work more today, or are you finished? Let's spend our last afternoon here, enjoying a picnic at one of my favorite spots nearby."

"I'm all done, Matt. In fact, I'm almost finished this part of the project in Banff. Thanks to you, I'm ahead of schedule. I'll be able to leave in a couple weeks."

"Leave? In two weeks? You mean go back to Calgary?" Matt seemed confused. "But didn't you say you'd be here in the fall, the winter? You'll be back later?"

"At the beginning, I figured my work would take me into the fall, even winter to complete, but it's gone much faster, thanks to you taking me into the field."

"Why not stay at your cabin where it's quiet to finish the rest of the project?"

"That's a nice thought, Matt, but I need the internet for digitizing my art. I also must spend time in Toronto with the publishers once they approve my submission."

"So, you'll be gone soon?" It wasn't like Matt to be so dense.

"Yes, you'll have one less critter to worry about." Fee tried to sound cheery, not succeeding. Matt's expression puzzled her. He looked like she'd announced that doomsday was two weeks from now.

"Sorry, I guess I didn't realize that you were leaving in a few weeks."

"Like you say, Matt, it's our last day here. Let's enjoy it. What should we take on our picnic?"

Matt pulled her to him in a fierce hug, burying his face in her hair. He turned away before Fee saw his face.

They flung a diverse collection of food in the backpack, anything edible without cooking, being the criteria. Matt led them up the main trail, but after two hundred yards, they veered off onto what appeared to be a narrow deer trail. It was all green shadows from the leaf-filtered light, and the lush summer overgrowth scented the air with wild strawberry.

"I hope I'm not Goldilocks meeting the three bears here. This seems like a perfect magnet for them." Fee fingered her bear spray canister on her belt.

"There isn't any fresh bear scat — could be they are further south, but let's keep our eyes and ears open. Stay close to me."

Fee admitted to herself that she felt safer hiking with an experienced field guy like Matt, and beyond that, he had his rifle with him. She hadn't brought her pistol. Who thinks to bring one on a picnic, anyway?

As they rounded a corner, Matt halted. Fee, tipping up her water to drink, slammed into him. He caught her before she fell into a thorn bush.

"You need brake warning lights." Fee grumbled as she snatched up her dropped bottle before it emptied all the water onto the ground.

Matt gripped her shoulders and turned her toward the scene in front of them.

A roofless log cabin stood in the middle of an English garden. Hollyhocks, roses, irises, lilies, and daisies ran riot around the cabin, and through its open door, which led to a pond where lily pads bloomed with dragonflies, their wings shimmering.

No human hand guided this garden now, only Mother Nature. The imported flowers, over the seasons, had won their place among the many native species. Their victory was celebrated in the flashes of red roses peeking from brambles, and the bearded purple irises standing erect next to twisted wild onion stocks. Shasta daisies danced with foxtails, while a rainbow of butterflies orbited them.

"I don't believe this. I feel like I've stepped through a magic door." Fee placed her hand on Matt's arm as if to grip reality.

He smiled down at her, enjoying the effect of the scene. "When I found it, I felt the same way. I'm not much of a gardener, but my mother is an avid one. I appreciate the labor needed to create a garden in the wilderness."

"Your mother is a gardener? You never mention her."

"No reason to talk about her. She left my father and me years ago, but I remember our childhood dashing through flowers in our garden where my mother spent her time."

"Aren't you an only child?"

"No, I have a younger sister, Barbara. She lives in California, as does my mother. Let's find a spot for our picnic."

Fee's curiosity was piqued, but she let the topic drop for now.

They found a shady spot under an old spruce tree to spread the blanket. It was above the cabin, allowing a panorama view of the garden and pond. Lunch was leftover biscuits from supper spread with honey and peanut butter, as well as the last of the breakfast trout, all washed down by instant ice tea.

"Matt, tell me a little about your sister, Barbara. Is she a scientist too?"

Matt scowled at Fee's persistence.

"She trained as a teacher, but married right out of college, has three kids. When Dad died, Babs was only nine, hadn't seen him for years. I doubt she remembered him."

"I shared my story, Matt. In fairness, I'd like to hear yours."

"I don't remember agreeing to a mutual recitation of family histories, especially when they are unpleasant." He stared off into the distance, and his fingers tapped his knee.

Fee felt as if he had physically left her, even though he was still sitting beside her. Wherever he had gone, it was not a pleasant place.

"I had a happy childhood until I was 11 years old when my mother got an offer of a temporary position as Head of the Natural Science Institute in California. She took my four-year-old sister, Babs, with her, and the next year she accepted a permanent position. My parents divorced then, and Mom and little Babs were gone for good."

"That's tough, Matt, and unfair. Were you close to Babs? She was much younger than you."

"I looked after Babs a lot because my parents, both university professors, were often late coming home at night. As her big brother, I protected her from scary spiders and neighborhood dogs. My cooking was either cheese macaroni from a box or hotdogs for supper, then we'd watch *Star Trek* reruns together. She snuggled up, her head on my lap, and went to sleep. Often, I tucked her into bed, calling her 'little bug in a rug.' I would have fought the Klingon Empire for her."

Fee's eyes were damp as she pictured Matt at eleven years old, all bony knees, skinny legs, and elbows, trying to fill in as the parent and protector for his little sister only to have her yanked away.

"What about your father? How was he after that? Did he help you deal with it?"

"All I remember was that he never laughed anymore, and then he got ill. He died of cancer a few years later. A retired uncle finished raising me."

Matt didn't mention that his Mom had wanted to come to the funeral and then have him come home to California with her. As a heartbroken fifteen-year-old, he'd decided that her concern was four years too late.

"Oh, Matt, I'm so sorry." She snuggled closer to him and squeezed his arm.

"Thanks, Fee, but its ancient history now." He turned to her, forcing a smile. "Let's enjoy this strange and beautiful place."

No doubt about it, Matt's childhood was still an unhealed wound. She could relate to that. "It's your life, Matt, but do you think it's time to visit your sister and mom? To reclaim your family ties?"

"No, I don't." He tried to take the sting away. "It's too nice a day and too special a place for my bygone sorrows."

Fee watched him rub his forehead and take a deep breath.

"All right, then who built this cabin, planted this English garden?" No point continuing a painful discussion — on their last day.

He sighed, relieved to focus on a more neutral topic. "Everyone makes up stories about it, but the truth is lost. The most popular story is that a pair of illicit lovers fled here from England about a hundred years ago, but no grave markers have been found."

Matt studied Fee while she sat with her hands under her chin, her elbows on her knees, a whimsical expression on her face as she imagined the lost lovers. She belonged in this secret place; her gray eyes, almost silver, were full of wonder and puzzlement. This was the beautiful, passionate woman who'd haunted his dreams all summer. Would she leave his thoughts too when she left?

Fee turned to see if Matt had relaxed, but his eyes were shadowed with thought.

Should they follow the example of those lost lovers and escape into the healing power of intimacy?

"In honor of those long-ago lovers, let's make love here today, do you agree?"

Matt grinned at her boldness and invitation. "No doubt that's the right thing to do, but on the condition that you agree to be musical."

"Musical? You mean sing and hum during... ?"

"Let's get naked, and I'll show you."

Despite their enthusiasm, it took time to strip off their hiking boots, clothes, and attachments like bear spray, plus Matt had to defend Fee's bare bum from a wasp showing too much interest.

"It seems simpler in the movies when they do this."

"Want to try something they don't do?" He reached for Fee's bare ankle and attached a bear bell, likewise to the other one. Tying bells to his ankles and wrists, he handed her two for her wrists.

"Fee, we need to make enough noise to scare away bears who might happen upon us while we are otherwise engaged."

"You mean our moans and groans aren't enough?"

Matt wrapped his arms around her and pulled her on top of him. The jingle-jangle of their bear bells scared away the creatures, but by the time they reached their climax, anyone nearby would be expecting an ice cream truck to be coming down the trail.

—*—

The light was fading fast as they exited the trail by the blind. The shorter days, crisper nights signaled the season's change.

"We must start back early tomorrow. 5:30 a.m.? Let's pack up tonight. We won't fish tomorrow morning if that's all right with you?" Matt suggested.

"No problem. Trout is safe from me for a minimum of a year. I appreciated a source of fresh food every day, but the trout need to invite other fish species to hang out with them. We could have used more variety."

"After we get back to our cabins tomorrow, we'll head to a steakhouse in the town of Banff that has filets that don't involve fish."

Fee didn't answer, and Matt stopped walking as he waited for her response.

"Matt, tonight is our last night together."

"Last night?"

"You were honest from the beginning that you're not interested in a committed relationship, and I accept that."

"Fee, I do have feelings for you, admire you. It's just that . . ."

"Let's not make this hard, Matt. I care for you too, likely I love you, but you don't feel the same way. I even understand why you can't, now that I know about your sad childhood. Let's make it a clean break when we return to our cabins."

"Couldn't we wait until you leave for Calgary, Fee?" His voice was husky.

Fee breathed slowly, controlling her reaction. What did she expect from him? A last-minute declaration of love? He hadn't argued, just asked that the affair go on a bit longer.

"I'll need recovery time before I return to Calgary. Before now, my fears of being left behind made me hold back on life. Not anymore. It'll be painful, but I'll heal and find someone who can love me back. Let's make this a night to remember."

Fee turned away and climbed the stairs of the blind, glad the dusk hid her damp eyes.

That night Matt's tender lovemaking was more than sensuous. He sought each curve, valley, dimple, and cleft, traced it with his fingers, then tasted it with his tongue until Fee went mad. It was like he wanted her very flesh to remember him. He entered her, building his rhythm as he gazed deep into her eyes. When she came, the tears rolled down her cheeks unchecked. Matt held her and rocked her in his sheltering arms until she fell asleep.

The morning sky clouded over to a new bruise purple, foretelling rain by noon. Packed, ready to leave, both stood to study the clouds.

"Let's try to reach the easier part of the trail before it rains."

"I'm packed, and I have my rain poncho ready. Let's go!" Fee stomped off, setting the pace.

Matt was glad of his long legs because Fee was traveling fast, climbing over the fallen trees like a mountain goat and striding up the slopes. It was like she was trying to escape. He wasn't sure if it was the rain or him. "Slow down, Fee. You need to pace yourself. We won't outrun the rain."

Fee lessened her pace. He was right. It wasn't possible to run all the way to her cabin, no matter how much she wanted to get the whole thing over. Last night had been bittersweet torture. Now she needed to be alone.

As they reached their usual rest stop at the stream, the rain came, pelting them, creating puddles. They huddled on a log under a tree eating crackers and cold chili from pouches. No one spoke. Twenty minutes later, they were back on the trail, the rain beating on their heads.

When at last they reached her cabin, Matt insisted on lighting the stove before he left. Once he had it roaring away, he turned to go, hesitated, then bent over, kissed her mouth hard, and then stepped out the door.

From the doorway, Fee watched his retreat, likely for the last time. His broad shoulders spread out his slicker like a sail whipped by the wind. When he disappeared, she closed the door. She stretched out on the bed, pulling a blanket up to her chin and then over her head. Let the world go away.

Chapter 23

Matt stood in Fee's small cabin. He'd knocked, but there was no answer. Her narrow bed was stirred up like a tornado had hit it. Her night had been no better than his. He straightened the blankets, burying his face in her pillow, searching for her scent like a rescue dog seeking a missing person.

Two weeks without Fee, and nothing was back to normal. For one, he should be proud he had, at last, solved the mystery of the elk population's dominance — a problem with the wolves' fertility rates. A new and rare invasive plant eaten by the small prey the wolves consumed was disrupting the female wolves' fertility cycles. It seemed that even predators sometimes need a helping hand in the romance department. But it was as if Matt didn't care.

Without Fee to tell the news of his success, to watch her face light up while she fired questions at him, laugh at her humor— the victory was flat, not worth a celebration.

Before Fee, he'd have headed to town to celebrate, probably contacted Angelique, who would feign interest in his accomplishment, and then they would finish off the evening with wine and meaningless sex. Now, that was the last thing he wanted.

On the wall, a sketch of the Rocky Mountains was askew. He sat on her bed and pulled Fee's sketch pad out of her backpack. He flipped the pages, and their time together came alive for him. The hut morphed from on fire to patched up again, the raven pecked at the cracker box, the animals, big and tiny, shy and ferocious, sprang at him.

Fee had even included humans in her sketches. There he was, his naked body facing away, arms raised, as he washed in the downpour, and there was her nude body, sleek with rain, in motion, dancing with abandonment and joy.

Next, a sketch of Geoff and he, bare-chested, pounding away at the deck, and also a waterfall she must have seen with Geoff. The next page exhibited the magnificent silver wolf she'd wounded, the dark, menacing wood around her, and the pack that had pursued them.

He flipped to the last page. In the background were two sets of bare feet on a blanket, bear bells tied to their ankles. In the foreground was a desolate log cabin surrounded by the untamed beauty of an English garden and lily pond.

Last night was his fourteenth night of hell since he and Fee had parted. He longed for her. He wanted to hear about her plans and — he just plain wanted her. Could he actually be crazy enough to allow his fears to make him abandon Fee to heartache, just to avoid it himself? If so, then he was a damn coward who didn't deserve her. He had to talk to her before she left.

I'd be insane to give up this beautiful woman. I love her, goddamn it! Give up my Fee, who faced wolves to protect me, who laughs at fire and physical discomfort, whose love of nature matches mine, and who loves me passionately?

No way in hell.

He set the sketchbook down and went searching for Fee.

—*—

Fee sat on a boulder facing the mighty Rocky Mountains. She wore a soft green sweater and tan jeans to combat the chill in the fall air. Her hair fell in wayward spirals and curls around her face like the burnished red leaves of the white ash tree beside her. Inside, her heart hurt, like it had been punched, and then stomped on.

All the fieldwork for her project was done, and she should be elated even if she was leaving all this natural beauty behind for a city. If only it were this wilderness she loved, and not Matt too. She meant what she said about not fearing abandonment anymore. She wished that her new view of life eased her present pain.

"I thought I would find you here. A sketch from this spot is on your wall."

Damn. Matt.

Matt strolled over and stood in front of her. His broad shoulders stretched his cream cable-knit sweater as he crossed his arms. His amber eyes bored into her.

"Is there something you want? Or is this boulder a restricted zone?" Fee's sarcasm didn't faze him. He moved closer.

"Yes, I want to ask you a question. Please stay there." He fell silent, gazing at her.

About half a minute ticked away.

"Matt, unlike that mountain, my time is limited. Please ask before I grow as old as it."

Why was he standing this close? If he tried to kiss her, she would make a run for it. She couldn't afford to ignite any feelings right now. Her fragile grip on herself wouldn't keep. Hell would be as cold as the Arctic before she'd let him see her tears — again.

"I'd be more comfortable if we were eyeball to eyeball for this question."

"Oh, for crap sake." Fee jumped up, clambered up the small boulder, and stood on top of it with her hands on her hips. "Is this good enough?"

Matt laughed. "Not what I had in mind, but it will do." He moved within a few inches of her, his eyes fixed on hers.

"Fiona MacRae, will you marry me?"

"What?"

"Fee, will you marry me?"

"Why?"

"Because I love you, my darling girl." He swept her off the boulder into his arms and sat her down on the huge rock.

He kneeled in front of her, meeting her confused eyes, "I've been an idiot, a bastard, but I've finally woken up to the fact that I don't want to lose you. Please forgive me for my stupidity, and the pain I've caused you. Fee, I love you." He grasped her hands and waited.

Fee looked at him, tilted her head to one side, "What makes you think I still love you?"

"Oh, God, Fee, have I destroyed your feelings for me? Hurt you too much? Please don't tell me that!"

"Well, my feelings are not totally dead yet, but you must work hard to revive them." She leaned over and kissed him as if testing her feelings. Matt swept her into his arms, his kiss worthy of a lot of consideration. She could feel his heart knocking against her chest.

"Fee, please, will you marry me?"

She reached up and stroked his cheek." I've loved you for a while, Matt, but this seems sudden on your part. Why the change of heart?" Her smoky eyes probed his.

"You've haunted me from the day I met you. You are in my mind, my dreams, and my blood. Don't leave. I need you in my life."

"Resistance is futile?" Fee laughed into his eyes.

"Yes. Now, for God's sake, woman, will you marry me?"

"What guarantee do I have that you won't change your mind?"

This was harder than he thought it would be. He should have expected that Fee wouldn't be easy to convince. What could he say next? She was owed the whole truth, brutal honesty.

"Fee, since I was eleven years old, I have avoided being hurt, avoided giving anyone the power to crush me. To be safe, my relationships end when I suspect any attachment forming, just like I ended ours. I'm new at commitment, and new to loving someone — you."

He placed one hand on his heart and the other on Fee's heart.

"I swear by my soul, by Mother Nature, the winds and fire, I will do everything in my power to stay yours for the rest of my life. Now, will you marry me, Fee?"

"Well, if you put it like that, yes, I will." She laughed into his lips as he claimed hers for good.

—*—

A few days later, Matt shared a beer with Duncan, who had made a special trip to congratulate Matt and Fee.

"Our life together will take planning and re-organizing. It'll take a fair bit of negotiation, even heated discussion."

Matt stopped speaking when Duncan chortled with hilarity to the point of choking and snorting his beer.

"Heated discussion? You're marrying Fee — *fierce, independent Fee*. You'll likely go toe-to-toe with her every other day."

"I welcome it. The biggest problem with my parents' marriage was that they never thrashed anything out. It was always resentful silence when there was a disagreement."

"No danger of that with Fee." Duncan jumped as he received a cuff to the back of his head. He hadn't seen Fee enter the room and come up behind him.

"Are you bad-mouthing me to my fiancé?" She laughed and kissed Duncan's cheek.

"Not at all — you are a perfect match. You have my blessing — and it's my sincere wish that you both survive the first year of marriage." He ducked to avoid Fee's swipe to the side of his head this time.

—*—

The harvest moon filled the horizon, gilding Matt and Fee's faces with a golden light as they gazed at the sky.

"You never get this kind of peace in the city. "

A wolf howled in the distance, another answered, soon there was a chorus of howls.

"You sure don't!"

"Let's join them." Fee threw back her head, blasting out a high-pitched howl that sounded more like a yodel.

Matt leaned over and nibbled her neck. "I have a better idea."

They turned to each other laughing, joining hearts for a wild life together.

The End

Sandra Baird

Sandra Baird

Sandra Baird has always been a risk-taker and a lover of new ideas. She comes from a family of storytellers in the old Celtic tradition of gathering around after meals, entertaining each other with tales of daring, and the wonders of the natural world. It was only a matter of time before Sandra took up the challenge of writing stories of love and adventure. She splits her time each year between Canada and Mexico.

Contact: cahoots417@gmail.com

Watch for new releases in ঙ꙰All's Fair in Love and Work series ঙ꙰

Tangled Vines

April 2020 Release

What would you do if you inherited both an Australian vineyard and a family secret that turns your life upside down?

What if you are a fiery young Italian chef from New York whose passion tempted you into having an anonymous one night stand with your smoking hot Aussie seatmate on the plane?

Then found out he hid a combustible secret from you? One that threatens your whole new life?

What if the reckless heat sizzling between you forces a course of action neither could have predicted?

Mile High

October 2020 Release

Kate, a former navy fighter pilot, is back where she longed to be, in the far North, flying small bush planes. She finds herself Christmas Eve on a rescue mission to save a stranded scientist. Worst yet, when she gets there, a storm traps her and the idiot in a situation that could mean death for them both.

It doesn't help that the guy is hot enough to melt polar ice and foolish enough to underestimate Kate's ability and determination to make sure that this mission isn't her last.

He is about to experience Kate's "Take No Prisoners" policy toward men who get in her way, especially men who think they can 'fire her jets.' This frigid winter night is about to get hot.

Want to know the **exact date** when new releases are available? Get in on **special promo prices?**
Just email Sandra Baird at cahoots417@gmail.com and say, "Keep me up to date!"—and I will add you to my email list.

Thanks for reading my book. I hope you enjoyed it! **Sandra**

www.ingramcontent.com/pod-product-compliance
Lightning Source LLC
Chambersburg PA
CBHW032006050726
47590CB00006B/2071